LAWLESS
SPACES

Also by
Corey Ann Haydu

OCD Love Story

Ever Cursed

LAWLESS SPACES

Corey Ann Haydu

SIMON & SCHUSTER BFYR

New York   London   Toronto   Sydney   New Delhi

SIMON & SCHUSTER BFYR

An imprint of Simon & Schuster Children's Publishing Division
1230 Avenue of the Americas, New York, New York 10020
This book is a work of fiction. Any references to historical events,
real people, or real places are used fictitiously. Other names, characters, places,
and events are products of the author's imagination, and any resemblance to
actual events or places or persons, living or dead, is entirely coincidental.
Text © 2022 by Corey Ann Haydu
Jacket illustration © 2022 by Emma Leonard
Jacket design by Krista Vossen © 2022 by Simon & Schuster, Inc.
All rights reserved, including the right of reproduction in whole or in part in any form.
SIMON & SCHUSTER BOOKS FOR YOUNG READERS
and related marks are trademarks of Simon & Schuster, Inc.
For information about special discounts for bulk purchases, please contact Simon &
Schuster Special Sales at 1-866-506-1949 or business@simonandschuster.com.
The Simon & Schuster Speakers Bureau can bring authors to your live event. For more
information or to book an event, contact the Simon & Schuster Speakers Bureau at
1-866-248-3049 or visit our website at www.simonspeakers.com.
Interior design by Tom Daly
The text for this book was set in Adobe Garamond Pro.
Manufactured in the United States of America
First Edition
2   4   6   8   10   9   7   5   3   1
Library of Congress Cataloging-in-Publication Data
Names: Haydu, Corey Ann, author.
Title: Lawless spaces / Corey Ann Haydu.
Description: First edition. | New York : Simon & Schuster Books for Young Readers,
[2022] | Audience: Ages 14 up. | Audience: Grades 10-12. | Summary:
While a highly publicized sexual assault case threatens to destroy her and her mother,
sixteen-year-old Mimi Dovewick tries to understand their tense relationship by reaching
out to the women of her maternal line through the journals they all kept.
Identifiers: LCCN 2021047141 | ISBN 9781534437067 (hardcover) |
ISBN 9781534437074 (paperback) | ISBN 9781534437081 (ebook)
Subjects: CYAC: Novels in verse. | Mothers and daughters—Fiction. | Sexual abuse—
Fiction. | Diaries—Fiction. | LCGFT: Novels in verse.
Classification: LCC PZ7.5.H424 Law 2022 | DDC [Fic]—dc23
LC record available at https://lccn.loc.gov/2021047141

To Christine Blasey Ford
To Anita Hill
To everyone who bravely speaks up
To everyone who isn't able to
To us all

and

To my pals at Southside Coffee
who in small and lovely ways
through chitchat and lattes and scones and community
helped me get through the pandemic
and take care of a kid
and write a book
I'd been trying to write for years.

Dear Reader,

Lawless Spaces includes material related to sexual trauma, sexual assault, sexual harassment, and generational trauma.

Please read with care, and step away if you need to protect your mental health. If you are in need of support, resources are listed in the back of this book.

With love,
Corey

LAWLESS
SPACES

Mimi, 2022

"A locker room is a lawless space," they say on the news.
Mom and I are on our separate corners of the big brown couch—

the one that Eric brought three years ago when he moved
in.
It is the kind of leather that
sticks to your thighs
even in the cold of December,
and makes you wonder if it is actually
leather
at all.

It is a lot like Eric.
Uncomfortable and
never
quite

                                        fitting in
to this house
with its yellow flowered curtains and
overstuffed armchairs.

It is a little like me
too
right now
not quite sure how I fit in
here
with them.

Or anywhere
with anyone.

While we watch, Eric
plays some card game on his
phone
at the kitchen counter,
and I stitch a dress into a T-shirt, gathering and snipping thread
and
reimagining who I might be
in it. The dress was too short, the kind of thing I wore
before,
but I miss the lace sleeves and the pale stripes and
how soft it was on my skin.

"Always thinking you're some
fashion designer," Eric
mumbles from the other room
like always. "Some famous
insta-whatever
girl."
I look for Mom to correct him and tell him to
shut up,
or at least tell him that the dream isn't
as ridiculous
as his frowning mouth
and rolling eyes
seem to suggest.

But.
Mom
is just
watching the news.

"Walter Bruce wasn't just talking in a locker room," the lawyer
with the short, neat haircut
says.

"Walter Bruce was on his set
and in his hotel rooms
and in their trailers
and in dark corners
at parties. And he wasn't just
talking.
He was
assaulting—"
"We're talking today about the comments
captured on tape,
the evidence we have,
the things he said that we have proof of. In the locker room,"
the reporter says.
She is blonde;
her mouth is tight.
Mom keeps calling her
a bitch,
which doesn't seem very helpful
at all.
And Mom's never called anyone

a bitch

before.

        (this isn't quite exactly true
        because
        once she called me
        a bitch,
        but we are both trying to forget
        that day, we are both trying to
        forget a lot of
        days)

"Hey, isn't that the guy you did the movie with
once?" Eric says,
wandering in from his spot in the kitchen,
sitting between us.
His legs slide apart,
his elbows find the tops
of the cushions.

I hate them there
and everywhere.

He shifts
and it's an earthquake
and it makes my needle slip and poke my thumb.
I gasp,
but no one hears.

I have been sewing my whole life—
outfits for dolls and stuffed rhinos and
now outfits for me.
And someday
someday
outfits for other people who can't decide
if they want to stand out or blend in—
other people who like loud patterns all mixed together in ways
that could seem wrong
but that I make right. Other people who
want their dresses to be the main event
and not
ever
what's underneath.

I have been sewing my whole life, but still
sometimes

I poke myself with the needle or make the wrong stitch in the
wrong place
and Eric always
notices, like he is adding up all the reasons I won't ever be
special.

"That's him, that's the guy," Eric says again and Mom
shakes her head.
Not as an answer
I don't think
more just a general
no
to it all.
She was an actress
once
but not now
and she doesn't like to talk about it, which he should
certainly
know. There is a long list of things
Mom doesn't talk about.

"And you believe a locker room is a lawless space," the lawyer on
TV repeats,
like she wants the anchorwoman
to hear herself.
"So the things he said there, the way he spoke about
those young girls,
isn't anything to—"

"It's not illegal to call someone
hot," the anchorwoman says with this
smirk. "Some of us
even
like it."

My needle finds my thumb again.
I want to turn the TV
off.
I don't want to hear those words
in this living room
with these people next to me. I decide to add a turtleneck to the dress
and another inch to the hem.

Mom's thighs unstick from the couch
loudly,
then re-stick.
They unstick again
louder.

"Oh my god, I hate that sound," I say
to no one,
really.

"Women have come forward," the lawyer says. "I am in
conversation with many
women who have come forward."
"*Anonymous* women," the anchorwoman says. Like anonymous means
fantastical;
like it means
paper-doll women made of cardboard.

She is not much of an anchorwoman,
really.
I don't think journalists can look so
smug
or draw so much attention to their
hotness. She is always wearing shirts that
hug

and

                        dip

and I know a lot about shirts that
hug
and

                        dip

and how careful
you have to be
about what people will

think.

              (right now my shirt is
              l   o   o   s   e
              but light
              which is also sort of
              bad
              because when your body is like
              mine
              and Mom's
              and that reporter's

you are really mostly always a little
bit
bad)

"It is what it is," the reporter says. "We can't police
lawless spaces."

The couch squeaks and
squitches against my thighs
when I try to get up from it,
like Mom's did,
the sound I hate but can't get away from,
and even just
here in my own home
I wish I could
quiet
my
body
and the way it
makes itself
known.

"Our bodies are lawless spaces," Mom whispers,
the only thing she's said
in ages.
She says it
right to me,
making sure I've heard her.
Her shirt dips

too. It always

does.

I heard what she said but I ask "what?" as if I haven't.

Eric
looks
down.

"We are the lawless spaces," Mom says
like it's the truth
she's been trying to tell me
all

along.

Mimi, 2022
Sixteen

This notebook is blue
and inside are three poems
about me
in my mother's curvy, swervy handwriting.
It is the beginning of something that she gets to
start and I guess it's my job to
finish—which is
the story of myself, or at least the story of
right now.

"Here," she says. "Happy birthday."
It is not a gift wrapped in silver paper,
it is not the things I wanted—
gold eye shadow and a ring light
for doing live posts.
It is just itself.
Soft-covered and lined,
crisp paper;
a lot of it. The poems she's written about me are
short
and mostly about who I was
when I was little and we were
close. I guess she doesn't know what to say about me
now. I guess I don't
either.

"Oh, right," I say. "These notebooks."
"I know traditions can be . . ." Mom sort of trails off. She hasn't
been great

at traditions.
Unless her going out to dinner with Eric
and not me
for her birthday is a tradition.
Unless her open-mouth kissing Eric at New Year's
is a tradition.
Unless Thanksgiving at Eric's mother's house
with Eric's mother's friends
where Eric's mother asks him why he can't find a woman
with less baggage

                                              (I am the baggage)
is a tradition.

"Mimi?" Mom says. "It's your birthday, so
you can be part of this
if you want.
Do you want it?
The notebook?
You remember about it,
right?"

I remember a lot of things:
tea parties with Mom in the attic, surrounded by notebooks
and the promise of some special day where I would have
notebooks
too. But instead there's this
non-moment
and Eric's footsteps echoing above
telling Mom to hurry up
and get this part of the day
over with.

Eric is
the kind of guy Mom thinks is
romantic

for wanting to move in after two months
and for touching her ass
in public.

"Happy birthday, Mimi!" he calls
now
from upstairs
where there used to be an aquarium
filled with tiny blue and green and gold fish
whose tails moved like
wind
and who were always in a sort of
beautiful
chaos.
Mom and I used to sit on the floor
and watch them
and wonder if it was all some sort of choreographed
dance
just for us.
Like maybe
there was magic
right in our own home.
But now there is a collection of weights
and a patch of fake
grass
to fake-golf on,
which is
basically
the most depressing thing a house could have in it
aside from
a mom who doesn't care
much
about you
and a live-in boyfriend she loves more than you,

which is also pretty
fucking
depressing.

Mom didn't even put up a fight
when Eric said we needed to get rid of the aquarium.
"But we love it," I said, in a whine I knew she hated but I
couldn't
help.
"I love Eric more than those fish," Mom said,
and I didn't know how to say
couldn't say
was too embarrassed to say
that it wasn't the fish
I loved
exactly
but those hours on the floor,
wondering.

I don't go in that room anymore.

"So I like, write poems?" I ask. Notebooks filled with
my mother's handwriting
and her mother's
and hers
have always been
around
in the attic with the now-empty
aquarium
and Mom's old headshots
and newspaper clippings of things
people said about her when she was in shows and
movies. They are alongside all the things I used to wear but
don't,

now that I know
what people think when you wear something that cuts

low

or hugs tight
or rides high on your thighs.

They are there in the attic,
the notebooks
with the other versions of ourselves we used to be but aren't
now.

I don't go to the attic
ever;
it's cold and also sort of
alive.

The boxes of notebooks
seem to hum.

I guess now that I think about it
there's a lot of places I don't go
in this house.

(and a lot of things we don't
say)

"It's what we've always done," Mom says. "The girls in this

family. When we turn sixteen—"
"And now I'm sixteen."
"And now you're sixteen. We're all connected. All of us. You've
seen. We look—"
"I know how we look."
On the mantel
above the fireplace
in the living room
is a row of photographs. They are all
black-and-white.
They are all
the same rectangular shape, framed in the same
gold frames that stand like soldiers saying
yessir, this is who we are.
The photographs are my mother and her mother
and hers and hers,
and all of them look
a little bit
the same with
golden-blonde hair and a body that is too
much
while also being too
little.
We are short and we have
curves—the kind people are comfortable commenting on
right
to
your
face.
There is a threshold I've found—
a type of body that is up for public discussion—
and it is mine
and my mother's and my grandmother's
and her mother's too.

(they think their words are
compliments:
you are so tiny! but also so

. . .

. . .

. . .

buxom)

"Well, so, we have these photos and we have
the notebooks
and that's our history,
that's
who we are." Mom's voice is
too quiet
and a little
shaky—
the way I sound
answering questions in class
about the Revolutionary War
or
chemistry. Maybe she doesn't quite exactly know
who we are.

"We have to take your photo,
too,
so we can make one of these for you."
I don't want
to be up on the mantel, looking like an inevitable
destiny. I prefer
the photos I post online,
with no ghosts
around,
no ancestors

putting me in some

category that I never asked to be in.

"Okay," I say, though, because what else am I going to say? I
don't know how to say
anything
to my mother
lately.
And besides,
saying no would make her
confused. *You love taking photos of yourself,* she would say.
But that's not it,
really.
I like being
the idea of a girl online
and not actually
this girl
here
in the kitchen
with a mom who keeps looking at her phone
instead of at me.

Online I do not have history. I only have
followers,
so many that a tampon company
wants me to do an ad for them.
Online
I am not
4' 10". Online
I do not have
breasts so big my shirts

strain. Online I have
friends and a really fun mom and hundreds of feet of space
between me and
everyone else,
which is how I like it, or how I've
learned
to like it.

"So we'll take a photo," I say now, though.
"And I'll write in a notebook. Poems, apparently."
"When you want to, Mimi."
"I've never wanted to write. I want to make clothes and I want
to
move somewhere far away where no one knows me except as
the girl with the cool account with the amazing clothes. That's
what I want."
"Well, your cool account has a lot of writing on it," Mom says.
"You write all kinds of things there."
And I'm about to tell her that's
stupid
because captioning one of my posts online
is hardly *writing*,
but what I mean
is that captioning one of my posts
isn't writing about anything true.
Not true the way it is
true
that Eric sometimes forgets to mention me
when his clients ask about his life.
Not true the way it is true that Mom asked if I was okay with
him moving in
and I said no
and he moved in
like

a day later.
Not true the way it is true
that I made my mother a skirt
from soft yellow material I thought she'd love
and
later
it ended up in the pile of clothes we donated
to make room for
Eric
and I never said anything because I knew
she'd forgotten
I'd made it at all.
Not true the way it is true that Mom looks out the window
or at her phone
or at Eric
when I talk
and never
at me.

So I guess I need
a notebook
to tell things to
because she's not listening
anymore.

"Can I post about the notebook? It's sort of
cool
and, like,
retro. And you know my followers love the whole
mother-daughter thing."
"It's not for that," Mom says. "The notebooks are for real life."
And I'm about to start a whole fight about
what it is to build an online following

and that being online feels more real
sometimes
than being
here
in this kitchen,
like right now,
where Mom bumps into me
and spills a tiny bit of hot coffee on my hand
and doesn't
ask if I'm okay,
if it
hurts.

But I don't start the fight. We don't really fight
anymore. You have to
talk to be able to fight.

So I shut up
and take the notebook
and write

this.

Mimi, 2022

"What did the rest of them write?" I ask
on our way out the door
as we gather up
purses and backpacks and snacks and
things we haven't yet said and might never
say.

"Oh, this and that," Mom says,
her jaw
tight and her purse slipping and sliding off her shoulder
so many times it seems like a joke,
except Mom doesn't ever joke
anymore. Eric doesn't like
the kind of jokes
we used to tell.

"What does that mean? Like, did they write about
the family? Or friends or boyfriends or just, like,
grocery lists?"

"You think I'm storing a hundred years' worth of grocery lists in
the attic?"
Mom sounds,
I don't know,
mad? But I can't decide what she might be mad at.
"I have no idea," I say. "That's why I'm asking." And maybe I'm
mad, too,
about
something or everything,

it's impossible to tell anymore.
Everything's just always
tense and

tight.

"There are things you don't want to say," Mom says, opening the
car door,
getting in. "So you write them down and put them in an attic
and then they can
exist and not exist,
they can be true and not true." She shrugs. She turns up the
radio
as if we aren't having a conversation,
as if some NPR reporter's voice
talking about climate change or
political poetry or
whatever
can drown me out.

"So you say these things and then put them in a box in the attic
and,
what,
wait for someone to
care?" I ask.

Mom turns the volume up
again. Their voices are
gentle but also
now
so

loud.

If I wrote down a bunch of
hard-to-say things and
waited for someone to care,
I'm pretty sure I'd be waiting

awhile.

"I don't know, Mimi," Mom says. She has to practically shout
over the radio.
"You all
say stuff online, so maybe you don't need a notebook,
but the rest of us,
we needed . . ."
The sentence drifts away before she can finish telling me
what
they all needed.

It is another
unsaid thing
in a pile of
unsaid things

except maybe this unsaid thing
is tucked into a box in the attic,
humming

the way secrets do.

Mimi, 2022

Then, the sleepy-sounding reporters stop talking about
foreign films and start talking about
that guy
again.
"So wait, was Eric right? Did you
know this guy?" I ask.

Mom's lips

                                        pucker

and she checks the rearview mirror like
a hundred times,
back and forth,
road to mirror, to road to mirror.

"I don't know, Mimi," she says
like I've asked her a question that is based on opinion and not
fact. We take a turn a little fast
and someone
honks.

"He seems sort of
nice. And cute, in those old pictures." I shrug.
"Do I know any of his movies?"

"I don't know, Mimi," she says
again. She keeps brushing invisible bangs
out of her eyes.

"I'm just trying to
chat," I say.
"You know I don't like talking about
those old days. You know that. So please stop
insisting on bringing it up
every five minutes."
"I only brought it up once. Right now."
"You know, I saw your account this morning and what you were
wearing—
it's not a good idea. I wasn't going to mention it until tomorrow
because it's your birthday,
but since you want to chat,
maybe that's what we should be
chatting about."

Last night I posted a photo
of me in my pajamas. They are
flannel. My hair was up in a ponytail and I
smiled.
I almost never
smile
in the photos. People don't always like
girls who smile too much. But they also don't like
when you smile
not enough.
I captioned the photo;
Dreaming of sixteen.
A thousand people liked it
and wished me a happy birthday
and like
two random dudes
said something gross.

"I've told you about buttons," Mom says. "When you're built

like us,
you can't wear
buttons. They
strain. And pajamas are . . .
they make people think about
beds. This is why
you don't have friends, Mimi. You don't
use your head. Other girls
don't want to be friends with
that."

It is the most Mom has said
in days.
Her eyes aren't darting around
anymore.
She finally has
my endless mistakes
to focus on.

"I forgot about
buttons," I say, which is true.
There are a lot of rules
about what to wear and when and also
how
and I forget them sometimes.
It has gotten so complicated that mostly
I make my own clothes now,
stitched together from things I used to wear
but now know not to
and things Mom stopped wearing when she met Eric and
things I find at thrift stores and fabric shops.
It's easier
this way,
wearing clothes that are

patchwork and peculiar,
the sorts of things
that people will notice before they notice
me.

Today: the frilly bottom of an apron affixed to
a thick woolen A-line skirt,
an Aerosmith T-shirt from Mom's discard pile,
made looser with silk panels sewn into the sides,
dark green and on sale, two yards for the price of one.
Now
all my shirts
have dark green silk panels,
dark green silk necklines,
my skirts inched down with dark green silk
borders.
Online they say I'm a fashion
icon, and ask me
how to do it. They find their own
dark green silk,
they all try to
wear what I'm wearing and be what I'm being,
except what I'm being is
someone trying to follow a list of unwritten,
always-changing
rules.

When we get to school, I look out the window and count the
number of girls
wearing button-down shirts.
Five at least, that I can see.
All five of them
have friends.

I don't mention it to Mom.

"Have a good day at school," she says. "A nice birthday. Sixteen
is
sure
something."
She puts her sunglasses down and they are so dark that I can't
see what her eyes
are doing underneath;
maybe they are looking at me
with something
like love
or
worry
or
wishing
but maybe
probably

she isn't
looking at me

at all.

I snap a selfie
with Mom's sunglasses and kissy face in the background,
which is a little like writing a poem
in a notebook
but is even more like
writing a dream
in my head
of who I want to be,

which is a girl whose mom has cool sunglasses
and an easy
way of being, the kind of mom that daughters call
"my best friend,"
the kind who
I don't know
takes you out for Thai food or
like
watches *The Bachelor* with you,
which are both things I have
pretended, online, that we do together.

no longer dreaming, just actually sixteen now,
but it is sort of
dreamy
I caption this photo
where I am the buttonless
blur
and my mom is the focus,
as if sixteen belongs
a little bit
to her.

Mimi, 2022

In photos
online
I am

smiling and
angled in this particular way
that makes my chin look
narrow
and my body's shape looks
right, while out in the world it is always
wrong.

In photos online I am
snuggling someone's puppy
or playing with ocean waves
or holding a sign for a protest that I might not actually
attend.

babe! they write under the photos
hotness
I wish I looked like youuuuu
love those jeans where are they from?
your ass tho!
I can't with your eye makeup.
can we hang soon?
sixteen and beautiful!

but also they write
slut!
16 or 25? your poor parents

ok but what do you look like in real life?
I'd do her
I'd do her if she lost a few
I'd do her if she gained a few
I'd do her, but only if I could tape her mouth shut.

In photos online
I am
someone people want to be
or fuck
or hate-follow
or root against or
for.
I am
sixteen and they say I'm pretty but also maybe
too pretty or
trying too hard or
full of myself or
inauthentic or also sometimes
such a role model and
exactly who I want to be when I'm sixteen
or
or
or
or
or

or

or

or

or

Mimi, 2022

No one at school knows it's my birthday because
no one at school knows

me

They know a little about the
girl online
and a lot about
the speed at which my breasts
grew
and they call me
Chanel or
Dior
sometimes
because of the clothes I make and the things I've said
I want to be,
and they also know something about
my not-exactly-stepdad Eric
because
once
he and my mom got in a fight

right   here

in the school parking lot
and he said we were lucky
that someone like him
wanted to be with

someone like her,
considering her   past
and it was pretty obvious
that I was the   past
and everyone watched me

walk   away

and actually it was the nicest some of them
had ever been to me
for a few days,
telling me I looked
nice, that they liked my
shirt or
whatever,
and sometimes sharing stories
of stepdads
or dads' girlfriends
who were also
assholes.

I tried to do what people do,
which is I think
smile and nod
and I don't know   hug?
but it felt too   hard
because it's different
with me—
Eric is   whatever
he's   fine
he   makes pretty good lasagna.

It's my mom

who doesn't act like a mom.
It's my mom who is
always changing the rules
and saying things that
cut.
Or saying
nothing,
which is maybe worse.
It is my mom who chooses Eric
and notices everything unlikable about me
and then
tells me about it.
It is my mom
who doesn't quite want to be
my mom.

And she's proving that point
today,
because when I get home
from a school day of fake smiles and stupid conversations about
where I got my shoes,
she's
                                                gone.

There's a note
about a trip with Eric
to some place in Arizona
that he surprised her with.
We'll be back Tuesday!
like it's normal to leave on your kid's birthday
on a surprise trip
for five days
without her.
Like I'm the one who's weird
for wondering why I'm not a girl who is worthy of a

nice dinner
or at least
a
fucking
cake.

Mimi, 2022

It's not the first time she's gone
like this,
but it's
the worst time,
and that's

something.

Upstairs
in the attic
the notebooks
hum some more,
and I think about reading
one
just to avoid being alone with my thoughts
on my birthday.

But. I don't read them. There's nothing in those notebooks
that could make this piece of toast
with peanut butter
for my sixteenth birthday dinner
okay.

Mimi, 2022

"You're that girl," some guy says
at Northside Coffee and Things,
where I go on Saturday morning
because I can't sit at home
alone
for another second
more.
Sitting at home
alone
reminds me of the quarantine,
almost three years ago,
when hours meant
nothing,
days meant
nothing,
and Eric was this unavoidable force who just kept
sighing
and turning the volume on the news up up up
and telling my mom that he couldn't *handle* being home
with a kid
for months on end.

I guess if I'd been
like
two
I'd get it.
But I was
thirteen
and barely spoke to him,
but still my mom would say,   "I know. It's hard."

like even knowing I
exist
is a burden.

So
I can't stay home remembering
that.

The guy talking to me now has dark hair and a "Clinton for
President" T-shirt
even though that was like
a hundred years ago.
"You are!" he says. "You're that girl."

"What girl am I?" I ask. And it's flirting,
maybe, but also
also
I really want to know
what kind of girl he thinks
I am.

"That online girl. You have the hot mom," he says.
Oh, I think.
And he must see it on my face,
that I wanted to be
some other kind of girl.
"I guess."
"She's not as hot as you," he says. "But wow
you're
tiny
like
teeny-tiny
I mean not
everywhere
but

are you even
five feet? Online you don't seem—"
"Okay," I say, wishing it was still just me and my coffee and the
window,
wishing the barista, Jake, with his white apron and swift smiles,
would come by to ask if I'm okay, if I want a sample of
banana bread or whatever.
"I'm not doing this right," the guy says.
"Nope."

I don't know, maybe I come here
hoping
some dude
will approach me.
That's probably what girls at school
think.
That's what my mom thinks
when I wear
tight pink sweaters or
skinny jeans
or sparkles on my eyelids.
And who am I to say
they're wrong?
Right now, I'm in a tight shirt I
saved from the attic pile,
with only a light cardigan
(no buttons!) hiding it.
Plus, I did my
hair and even my
makeup, because I was going to take
some
photos for my account, so
I guess this is
what I wanted.

I put down my mug.
I recross my legs
so that they are angled toward him.

This is
what I am good at.
This is
pretty much all I'm good at.

He's   cute.
Better
than the people in my DMs
who want to ask about my
bra
or
what I think of guys with big
dicks
or who just say
hey
and wait for me to
do the rest.

"I like your posts," he says. "They're smart.
And you're cute. And I'm sorry for being so
weird. I've never met someone
famous."
"I'm not that smart," I say, a reflex, and he
squints.
"And I'm really not famous at all," I try.
"My name is Clinton," he says, unsquinting.
"Like the T-shirt," I say. And he looks at his chest.
He's forgotten what he's
wearing
and right away I'm

bursting with jealousy
at not knowing every second
of every day
what is on your body
and how everyone
feels about it.
"Yeah, but also
I wish she'd won."
"Me too," I say. "I was ten and—"
"I know," he says. "I read your post on it."
And I want to say that reading my post on it
isn't the same as actually knowing how I feel about it
or anything,
but maybe that's not true.
Maybe I said all I had to say.
Maybe the photo of ten-year-old me
in a pink pussy hat
is the whole
story.
Maybe he knows me
as well as he thinks he does.

Maybe
he knows me
better than I know myself
anymore.

Mimi, 2022

On the walk home from Northside
someone stops me. It isn't a cute boy in a Clinton T-shirt.
It's just a
woman.
She's not old or young or anything. Just wearing a down jacket
and a striped scarf
like everyone else.
"Wow, you are short!" she says, having tapped me
on the shoulder.
"Oh. Yep. I am," I say.
I am wearing boots with three-inch heels
in the hopes that
maybe
today
no one would
notice.

But they always do. It is always first
my height
and then after that
my boobs
and then maybe
something about my hand-embellished jeans or patchwork scarf.

Or maybe,
like Clinton,
that they know me from
online.

"How tall *are* you?" she says. She probably does all kinds of
normal things like

feels nervous dining inside still, and
wears one pair of pajamas too many nights in a row, and
forgets what happened in the last chapter of the book she's
reading, and
wakes from a dream, confused about whether it was real or not,
but this thing she is doing now is such a weird
weird
thing to do—
telling a person
about the reality of their own
body,
and it happens a lot, but still
every time
I wonder
why and also
how.

Online
I am
any height, not necessarily
street-stoppingly short,
and I go barefoot
in those photos.
I don't need the heels;
I just exist.
And yes, they all
comment,
but it's about other things that feel
somehow
less
embarrassing.

Sometimes even the size of my breasts feels less
oppressive
than the fact of being
too short to reach any cupboard anywhere, too short to look any
taller than a
fifth grader.

"Not very tall at all," I say to the woman
and she laughs
but looks like she really still wants an answer
but I'm not going to give it to her
and I'm not going to keep walking in pace with her
so I
walk fast
and take turns I don't need to take,
which is fine
because no one is home waiting for me

anyway.

Mimi, 2022

Is this your mom? this girl from school,
Sadie,
asks online,
under a photo she's tagged me in
of a woman who looks
just
like
me

and the director from the news who is
Walter Bruce

and his arm is around her shoulder
and she is
wincing
like it hurts
but not the way something like a slap
hurts
more the way the quarantine
hurt
like you were
stuck
and there was no way to
get out.

And I mean
yeah
of course it's my mom
not just because her face looks like my face,

her smile
a little sorry
in the same
way,
but also because the photo is captioned
Tiffany Dovewick,
formerly anonymous accuser,
steps forward.

Mimi, 2022

My whole body
coils up
like armadillos do when they're scared.
It's called
volvation;
a fact I know from back when I was a kid and I thought I'd be a
zookeeper.
I learned everything there was to know about animals,
but then
I don't know
Mom put the aquarium away and gave the fish to our neighbors
and

I don't know

I stopped. I focused on sewing and photos and
seeming okay.
But some of the facts
stayed
and I think of them in times
like
this.

I am an armadillo, but everyone thinks I'm some girl
who has answers to these questions
that I definitely don't have. So I say nothing and everyone else
answers for me.

holy shit yeah of course that's
oh man, her mom, the hot one
she was famous too? the mom?
Mimi's not exactly famous, her mom was at least an actress
famous for something
real
well now she'll be famous for this

I try to rearrange the world
in my head
because none of this makes sense. Mom used to tell me
everything
before she did it. She showed me photos of a car
before she bought it,
and she let me help her pick out her earrings
before a date,
and we'd decide
together
what we would eat for breakfast on the weekend—pancakes
or bacon and eggs.

I text Mom, because she isn't texting me, isn't telling me
anything:
Remember when I used to help you pick
the color of your car? When you wouldn't
dream of deciding without me? And now you just—
I mean
is this real?
Are you accusing Walter Bruce of
something? Were you ever going to
tell me
or ask me what I thought?

It's almost exactly what I said to her
when she told me Eric would be moving in
after I said no. I brought up
Sunday breakfasts and how my opinion used to matter
and she said,
"This is my *life*, Mimi," like it wasn't mine
too. My fingers and toes go
cold,
feeling this lost way again, feeling small and silly and
unseen.

I don't know,
Mimi,
she texts back, which is
impossible,
she *does* know
whether or not she
like
reported
an assault.
The notebooks reminded me
she goes on,
and told me
and I got wrapped up and
have you ever known something was
true
but also really needed it to
not be?

It's weird how the words   swim
and cling to my heart
in all the ways that
hurt.

Because

I do know
about true things you wish were untrue
like how it is true
that Mom didn't come to the science fair when I was
twelve
because she said I was never going to be a zoologist or any other
kind of scientist
anyway.
And it is true that she didn't help me buy a dress
to the ninth-grade formal
because she was dating Eric
and he asked her to help him shop for
couches
and she said that was a
pretty big deal.
So I wore something
too small
that made too many people
raise their eyebrows at my
breasts
and later Mom said I should have known
better
but what I want to know is
how
if she never bothers to tell me
anything?
I know about true things that you wish were
untrue.
Like how I told her Eric didn't like me
and she didn't deny it but instead said
he was going to try his best to figure it out
and
now we're living with him and his
always-a-little-wet hair and his
always-a-little-mean comments about how lucky we are

to have him.

Like it is true
that she is gone
and I am here
and I am sixteen and maybe another kind of sixteen-year-old
would throw a party
or something,
but I don't go to parties
anymore. Like it is true that she knows why
but pretends she doesn't.

I know
about true true true things
that you wish were
untrue

but I do not know
(it turns out)
much about
my mother.

Mimi, 2022

They find
my phone number.
Hers too, I'm sure,
but I wouldn't know because she's
not
here.

I answer
once.
"Mimi?" a chipper voice says. "I'm so glad I caught you! I have a
few questions about
your mother."
I hang up,
but the phone keeps
ringing.

what am I supposed to do?
I text Mom.

And she
doesn't answer,
and I think this is an emergency,
but I guess even
in an emergency
I'm on my own.

I don't have a dad or
aunts and uncles or even just
a best friend

who can swoop in and
save me.

There are a few girls at school who I
sit with at lunch
and we talk about
my social media
and their boyfriends
and how much we hate
the principal.
They ask if I can teach them how to
jazz up their T-shirts, if I can show them how to
cut the collars, undo the seams, make something they like
into something they
love.

But I wouldn't know how to say to them:
my mom accused some famous guy of something
awful and she's gone and no one is telling me
what to do and I'm
scared.

I think
other girls
tell each other secrets
about boys or bodies or moms or this feeling here, this
heart-rushing, hand-shaking, world-shifting
dizziness. But not me.

A few years ago I told my mother
my biggest secret and
now I keep them all to myself.
It's easier that way.

I guess
Mom's secrets aren't so unreachable, actually. They are
in the attic, scrunched into notebooks that are lined up in a box
marked in Sharpie with
her name.
The past just
sitting around
waiting for me to
learn it.

Except
I can't
because my heart just keeps thumping out the present
why did she leave why did she leave why did she leave
and
I can't trust her
and
it is always this way
and there isn't any room to learn the past
when the present is so

t   h   i   c   k

and
real
and here.

Mimi, 2022

More reporters
find me on social media
and my account is flooded
within an hour
with requests to talk and phone numbers to call and questions
that
I don't want to answer and also
can't answer
because
my
mom
isn't
here.

I try to just be an armadillo, but it's
hard
because it's so quiet and also so
noisy
and I am trying to hold on to something
that maybe doesn't exist. I remember being
three and four and five
and trying to hang on to the monkey bars, but my hands were
too small and the bars were
too slippery,
and right now I am that little girl
and the way I want my life to be is the monkey bars,
except they might not even be there
at all.

And I am also
an armadillo.

And then it is
eight o'clock and nine and ten
and my mom still hasn't texted me back
and my heart is racing with all the not knowing what to do
and all the wishing she were here
and all the wondering why she isn't
and in a zoom of worry and wonder and waiting I say
out loud
to no one, to the couch, I guess,
"Fine, I'll go," and
I get up
to the fifth step of the ladder
to the attic,
where the notebooks are waiting for me.

But then Clinton texts,
and it is the perfect excuse to
stop the climb.

He says something about
the book he's reading
in English class at his school.

I'm not looking for
I try,
but I sound
ancient.
I don't date people
but he hasn't actually asked me
on a date.
I'm not who you think I am

and that sounds stupid too,
dramatic,
like something the online me might write,
but I'm not online
and it feels
weird.

I want to say something
Notebook Mimi would say;
something at least a little bit
real.

What's your favorite book?
is what I end up texting back.
It's what Mom once said was the perfect question
to ask a guy,
and so here I am, asking a guy,
even though I hate when Mom tells me
how to be with guys
and what kind of girls guys like
and how to better be
the kind of girl
who guys like.

But what's weird is
I actually sort of want to know
the answer.

Mimi, 2022

The house feels
huge
and honestly a little
scary
when everyone outside of it is waiting for me to do something
or
say something.

I write texts to a few of the girls
from school.
Grace, who is always asking how I get my hair to
bounce,
and Sophie,
who does great impressions of our math teacher.

I'm having a weird
my mom did something and I'm
what would you do if
have you seen the photo
I'm alone. I need help. what do I
I'm scared.

I don't send them.
I never send them.
I imagine Sophie and Grace copying and pasting the texts to
a hundred other people,
the wildfire of saying something you actually really mean
and don't want everyone to hear.
I know

about private things made
public, about things that get sent around
without your control,
shifting
everything, and trapping you
inside
of that change.

I know about staying quiet,
staying safe,
making sure people know exactly what you want them to
and nothing
more.
It's best
to be the girl online who looks
dreamily
off camera sometimes,
at nothing or everything or to some other place
she wants to be.

It is better
obviously
to be @MimiDove
than to be
Mimi
Dovewick.
It is safer
there.

Except
people are reaching out to @MimiDove
for comment.

And all I want
is to stare dreamily
off camera
to a place that isn't
here or

now.

Mimi, 2022

Mom isn't here.
She isn't responding.
Minutes and hours just
pass until my head and my heart feel like they are in some kind of
traffic jam.
The whole world (except Mom) is
shouting at me
through comments and texts and phone calls and
news alerts on my phone:
Tiffany Dovewick Tells Her Story
Tiffany Dovewick: A Timeline of Abuse
Is Tiffany Dovewick a Reliable Source?
Tiffany Dovewick: Just Trying to Get Her 15 Minutes Back?

I try to pretend the headlines are about someone else.
Otherwise the traffic in my head gets
louder;
more crashes,
more chaos.

I want to be small and unknown, but
it feels like they are all begging me to
Say Something.
Hundreds of messages flooding my photos,
asking me to
comment
comment
comment

Say Something.

Past midnight,
the traffic jam of my head and heart gets so loud I can't sleep or
eat or
be
and I look for images or words that I can put out there, that will
do something
that will make it stop or
at least start differently.

I take a photo of the women on the mantel,
but that's not right,
and neither is the picture of me on my lawn looking at the
moon alone.
I try taking photos of
my hands,
my arms,
the flowers Eric got Mom for
my birthday when he got me
nothing,
the television talking incessantly about
my mother. None of the photos are
right.

I swipe through hundreds of photos on my phone
of me and Mom and me alone and me at a school concert
standing next to people who might be my friends if I told them
anything at all,
and in the mess of those photos
that say nothing about anything,
there is one that says
something.

In it
I am
twelve and shaggy-haired and Mom is smiling and lipsticked
and we are
wearing the same T-shirts that say
"Believe Women"
that Mom bought us even though she never really explained
why
but it seemed simple
enough
to believe women.

In the photo my hands are on my hips and my chest is
out
and I am smiling a smile that I don't think
belongs to me,
at least not anymore.
Maybe it has gone the way of
the one lost mitten from my favorite pair
or to the secondhand shop where Mom brings everything we
have outgrown—
my scooter, her printer, the champagne-colored bed frame for
the
double bed she used to
let me sleep in sometimes
when I was
sad
and she was
single
and we were
something that maybe we never really actually were.

Now she sleeps in a

king
with Eric
and I smile with my mouth closed
and my mitten
is
still
gone, I guess.

A throwback photo to let you all
know where I stand,
I write.
We should definitely
Believe Women
but also
who could blame anyone
who thought my mom
was a
babe?

I hit post.
I mean it to be
a little cute.
I mean it
mostly
to make the feeling in my chest and the way it collides with the
beating of my heart
go away so I can sleep or think or loosen up my grip on the
couch cushion
that I have apparently decided is an anchor keeping me from
floating away.

But immediately it is so
fucking
obvious

that the photo, the post, was a mistake.

It is hard to do and say the right things
from an empty house that echoes when you
breathe.

A thing I don't say online
or even really in my head   much
is that it is
lonely
when I remember that other people have two parents and I have
like
one half of one
and it doesn't exactly feel like a
coincidence
that my dad never cared to know me and my mom is sort of
leaving
too.
I mean,
that must be
for a reason,
you know?

Everyone leaves Mimi Dovewick,
but
@MimiDove
is someone beloved,
someone who is the right amount of
nice and pretty and sweet and funny and everything people like,
except
not today,
because today I
did it
wrong.

Victim-blaming her own mom
this is what's wrong with today's youth
She goes to my school and she's so weird
she goes to my school and they're both pretty hot
Her mom dressed her like this? She's a CHILD
she needs to put away those—
like mother like daughter, I guess, look at them both
forcing their
tits
in your face
don't call them tits
when she's only, like, ten here
attention seekers
both of them
clearly
they
love
the
attention.
Obviously this woman wasn't assaulted
if her daughter is so
what's the word
what's the word
you know. You know. We all know.

Mimi, 2022

Mom finally calls at ten the next morning
and I'm asleep on the couch
when the noise of my phone ringing
wakes me up in a terrible
hollowing
whoosh.

"Mom! Oh my god, finally. Are you okay? What do I—"
"What were you thinking, Mimi, posting that picture, saying
Walter Bruce
couldn't help but
do what he did?
What kind of
daughter are you?
Do you have any idea what you've done, what I've been
dealing with?"
"That's not what I said at all! I was trying to say—I didn't know
what to—"
"I raised you better than this. I did everything for you.
I didn't even want you,
and now you're on the goddamn internet
telling the world that I
deserved it."

She waits for me to
respond,
but I am lost in the sea of the words
I didn't even want you,
which are so terrible they must be

true;
the kind of true you always knew was
true.
The words are an ocean, and I am
a girl who doesn't
quite
know how to swim.

Other people,
with best friends—
maybe they would tell them about the things their mother said
when she was too tired to remember not to say it.
But I am not
other people
with best friends
and I take those words
I didn't even want you
and lock them deep
d
e
e
p

down so that they can be a secret,
even to me.

I put them in this notebook
here
because I guess I want to be
like the other girls on the mantel
and have a place to store
the things you can't say out loud
but that you

maybe

want someone
someday
to
hear.

> (In the same flash of
> wanting,
> I have the feeling of wanting
> to be seen
> and wanting to hide,
> and maybe that's what a secret
> is.
> The delicious and awful space
> between hiding and
> wanting to be found.)

"I was trying to make it
like
not such a big—" I try. Then start again. "I mean, I said you
were
hot
because you are. You're beautiful and you know
how guys get
about your
body."

"How do they get, Mimi?" Mom asks, and she is so mad she
almost sounds
like a mom.
"They can't control themselves," I say, because she has said it
to me
and that's what she said after
everything
after that one party and that one picture,
and I have tried to
listen
when she tells me the rules about
button-down shirts and
V-necks and tight sweaters,
even though she doesn't really quite
follow any of those rules
herself,
always showing up places in
tiny skirts and
strappy tank tops
and red lipstick.

I guess
it sounds different
when I say the things she has said.

"Where did you even
come from?" Mom asks in this small,
awful
voice,
like she really and truly doesn't know the answer.
"I was trying to
help.
I didn't know,
I don't know,

when everything happened with me, you said—so I thought
I was doing the right thing."
"You're my daughter, you should support me, and, goddammit,
all I wanted was time with
Eric.
Time away to be prepared for this
fight,
to get myself ready to go after this
man,
and you can't even give me that
small
thing
that I need. I ask for
so little from you,
Mimi,
and still
here we are. I just want
five minutes with the person that I love
where I don't have to be—"

She doesn't finish the sentence because Eric
(the person she
loves,
I guess)
takes the phone from her, tells her to
breathe,
tells her it's okay, that she can talk to me tomorrow,
that he will help her fix this mess
that her daughter made.
He does not
say anything to me,
not even goodbye,
just hangs up the phone.

Mimi, 2022

We used to be

close.

I try to make it all make sense, all the bits and pieces and scraps of
us:
that she used to braid my hair for me,
and would
hum
along with the movement of her fingers;

that she
sighed
when I first needed a
bra;

that we took a vacation together
once
to this tiny house on a lake
and we picnicked on the beach for dinner
and went swimming all day,
every day,
and it was perfect,
except she kept saying,
in this sort of wistful way,

that it was the kind of place you were supposed to go with a
family,
and I'd thought we
were
a family;

that sometimes,
not very often
lately,
she checks on me
before she goes to bed
and stays in the doorway,
letting light peek in,
but that it's a secret,
a little bit of love or
whatever
that I'm not supposed to see;

that she takes photos with me for my account
and looks right into the camera
with this
smile
that dazzles,
and she says,
"Sure,
fine,
tell them whatever you want to
tell them,
Mimi," when I ask if I can write a post
about the unbreakable bond
of mothers and daughters.

Mimi, 2022

Monday is the last day of school before break,
a weird little island of a day
where all we do is watch movies
and everyone's talking about
ski trips
and stockings and silly little siblings with notes to Santa.

I'm just happy they are not discussing Walter Bruce,
though it feels like maybe they were
warned
not to,
because some of them look at me
extra long
and lick their lips like they have to remind their mouths to shut
up.

I used to think
a lot
about friends—the way people have them, the way I used to
have some,
and how
now
I just have lunchtime and
the vaguest details about some of the girls
who think it's cool that
once
I got paid to post about lip balm, and another time
a guy who used to be on the Disney Channel
commented on my picture

that I was
cute.
I don't think that's the same thing as
having friends.

The thing about looking
like your mom
when your mom is
Tiffany Dovewick
is that Tiffany Dovewick is the woman who is beautiful and
wrecked,
whose hair looks like a mermaid's
and who,
when you are thirteen years old,
kisses her boyfriend on the mouth in public
in the school parking lot,
even,
even if that boyfriend
is someone's dad,
and even if that someone's dad
used to be married to my classmate's mom.

So, I mean,
no.
I don't really have friends.

Now I just have
secrets
and things that may become secrets
and things I wish we could have kept
secret.

Sophie tells me she likes my

shirt, an old camp T-shirt I strung ribbons through.
She asks if I can make her one, someday, from this Taylor Swift
T-shirt she has,
and I say "sure yeah okay" while she tries to decide if she should
say anything
else.
Grace says my mom is her
new hero,
and she gives me this look like we are in on some
secret together, but we are
not.

This girl we sometimes sit with, Maya, asks if I'm okay.
She tilts her head and says it all
quiet,
like it is safe to say something
real.
I
don't answer.
She is always asking questions
that I can't answer
about who I am or what I feel or what
being me
is like.

The rest of the day is

quiet.

After dinner,
which is mac and cheese because I only know how to make

mac and cheese,
Clinton texts and asks
if I want to go for a walk,
which is probably code for
"hook up in the woods"
or
"smoke weed in some parking lot
somewhere,"
so I just
ask,
a real walk?
and he says,
what other kind of walk is there?
and I say,
I don't know, "walks" that are just ways to
get fucked up
or
get naked
or
whatever.
He calls me jaded and I call him
sketchy,
and maybe neither of us mean it, or
maybe we both do,
and actually I do
sort of
want to go on a walk,
because online everyone is still talking about my
post
and people from school are letting the world know that I wore
a tight T-shirt today (Sophie probably will not
                        still want me to make her a shirt like mine.
                        No one wants to be noticed
                        like this. I thought ribbons were

safe. Sort of demure and
girly, in the good way.)
too
and that I seemed
smug,
which is
I mean
smug
when I'm living alone with
a bunch of ghosts in the attic that I'm too scared to
confront
and I don't even have a friend to talk to, so the only person I'm
texting
aside from my MIA mom
is some guy I met at Northside
who doesn't even know my middle name or
whether I'm a dog or cat person.
But sure.
Okay.
Smug.

The mac and cheese
tastes like
shit
and my stomach swirls from that or from
the rest of it.
And I am an armadillo
again,
curling in on myself so that they can't get me,
can't see me,
can't judge anything about me or even know I'm here,
which would be,
I mean,

that would be the dream.

I want to think about nothing,
or maybe about Clinton's biceps or
whatever other girls are allowed to think about,
but what I can't stop thinking about is that my mother is being called
some kind of feminist hero
by people who would maybe be appalled to know
some of the things she has said about my
body.
And who also
once
not that long ago but also maybe forever ago
told me
the photos
after that one party
were pretty much my fault,
and who is,
I have to say it even though it is the most obvious fact:
not
here.

I'm scared that if I go for a walk with Clinton, I'll say
all of that
and more
because it is all thrumming in me,
so close to the surface that it is making it hard to breathe or
think or

be.
But I don't say things like that

out loud
or online
or even
really
in my head usually,
so I don't know why I'm saying it
here, except that the house feels cold but also sort of
wet and humid and I feel those things too. Loneliness is just an
impossible mix of
weathers, maybe.

I wonder if the notebooks explain
why it feels hard and also scary to say yes to Clinton and a walk,
or why I think a walk can't be a walk and why my body thinks it
is both summer and winter
at once
when I am scared and alone and why ribbons are sometimes
sweet and sometimes
slutty depending on who's wearing them.
I wonder if the notebooks explain why I am learning about my
mom
from the news
and why she isn't here
and what it is that would make her
come
back.

I can't walk, I text Clinton at last.
I have to read.
He doesn't say anything for a while,
but then he says okay,
and after an even longer pause he says,
The walk was just

a walk
I know when shit is
happening
a walk sometimes
helps
and I guess it seemed like maybe
some shit
was happening.

I guess Clinton's seen the comments
or heard my mom's name on the news
and that makes my face,
my body,
flush with being too known. I want to force his gaze back
to the girl he saw online,
stitching her own sundresses and hugging her
mom,
and cradling a coffee mug in the perfect shade of
mauve
on a snowy day.
Still. I guess maybe
I don't hate
that he said
The walk was just a walk
all
casual
and stuff,
just a tiny way to say that he
sees me
and sees that maybe something's really wrong
and that maybe he's even saying that all that wrong
could be
okay.

(It is probably not okay.
I am probably not
okay. Only the girl with the mauve mug
and homemade sundress is
okay.)

Mimi, 2022

The New York Times
has an article up
about my mother and whether she is
good enough to be a good victim
or something.
Eric sends it to me with the commentary:
Look what you've done.
You don't know anything
about anything.
And that is,
yeah,
I mean, that's true, I didn't know,
for instance,
that Mom didn't want me.
And I didn't know that she was going to tell the whole world
all about who she is
before she ever thought to tell me.

I don't know
even
when they are coming back or if the phone will
ever
ever
ever
stop ringing.

And I start to type those things to Eric, but then remember
who
he

is.
And I stop.

My finger hovers over the link to the article,
but the answers aren't there,
they are
humming
upstairs in those boxes, just like always. The sound of secrets
is louder
than you'd think.

And loudest, still,
when you are
alone
and
haunted.

Mimi, 2022

The notebooks have always been here
in boxes in the attic—
dozens of them.
Each one starting on the sixteenth birthday.
My mom,
my grandmother,
my great-grandmother,
and on
and on and
on.

They've sat there like a promise. Or a
threat.

But because they have always been here,
I have never cared to read them.

The things that are familiar and constant
are never
mysterious and interesting,
which is why it's so easy to fall in love with
people we don't know
and so hard to keep loving
the people we do.

Mimi, 2022

It's funny how short
the walk up the stairs to the attic is.
And how
easily the boxes
open.

I'd always thought it would be a whole
production,
with scissors and worries and rituals of some kind
or another.

"Someday, someday," Mom always said
about reading them,
like there would be a sign from the gods
or something. But really all I needed
was the unbelievable heaviness
of being alone.
Of being filled with my own
unsayable secrets.

I don't know where to start, so I start

with Mom,
of course.

Tiffany, 1999

Sixteen

"Streamers are for losers," Rachel says.

But I'd wanted them—
streamers and balloons—
the way I had when I was a little kid
and my mother did things
like hang up decorations
and bake cakes.

But sixteen is
instead:
a black dress,
and dark rooms, and
the kind of music that
lives in your bones,
rattles them so that you remember they are holding you

together,

makes your parents cringe away from the noise,
helps you forget
to remember
who touched you where and when   and how.

Sixteen
is Bud Lights in the basement
and
performing Juliet on the balcony

in just my bra
because Bud Light told me to
and
waiting for
seventeen.

Sixteen
is a first kiss that no one will ever know
was a first kiss;
sixteen is kissing Tyler, who plays lacrosse and has bleary eyes
when he drinks;
and it is his lips on mine,
and it is still thinking about Juliet,
and Romeo,
and balconies,
and poison,
and the tragedy of loving someone you'll never really
have.

Sixteen is the way a kiss ends
before it's really over
and wanting it to mean something

more

than it ever actually will.

    Sixteen is the way streamers droop at
    the end of a party
    and Rachel's vomit in my bed
    and my gaze at the ceiling,
   still wishing we had had streamers
   and balloons
   and cake,

all the things that make a party light and fun
instead of whatever this
was.

Sixteen is

hoping maybe before I fall asleep
it will all feel   different

Mimi, 2022

I put the notebook

down.
And stare at the ceiling instead.
I've never heard of Rachel
or Mom's sixteenth birthday
or some guy named Tyler

and I realize
with a flash of

something

that I am not ready to think of her
like this
like me
like a teenager who wants more than what she has
like a girl who is being told who she is
like a person who is trying and trying and trying to be
someone
anyone.

I want a few more moments where my life is sort of
small

and
mine
and it doesn't matter
who hurt her when
or what happened with Tyler
or Rachel
or Walter Bruce
or

anyone
because what matters is
now
and the way now

hurts.

So I put the Tiffany notebooks
away
and start again
with someone else's secrets
that can't hurt me or
unhurt me
as much.

I open a box and find the notebooks of my mom's mom,
my grandmother,
who I met
once

and then never again
even though she lives two hours away
in a home covered in
vines.

(Still, Mom's notebooks sit
right next to me,
doing a quiet sort of
haunting.)

Wendy, 1971
Sixteen

When I come downstairs I am hoping
perhaps
for something like a celebration.

Cake
maybe
for breakfast!
Like we did when I was young.

Or a present?
Something shiny or sparkly
or soft.

I would have settled for a card.

But instead there is just
this notebook and
cold cereal
and my mother in a strange position in the kitchen,
bent at the waist,
her forehead on the
counter.

"Mom?" I say. "Are you okay?"
And Mom
doesn't pop up,
doesn't put on a smile and tell me it's
fine.

"Lately," she says,
"your birthdays just remind me of
her."

"Her?"
Mom is fuzzy from time to time. Maybe it's from
wine or from
not sleeping enough or I suppose from
the way things are right now—
the War and the broken country and the way it makes everyone
a little
fuzzy.

"Wendy," Mom says.
"I'm Wendy," I say.
"Right," Mom says, the cloud sort of lifting. "Yes. You're
Wendy."
"Are you okay?" I ask.
And she just
shakes her head and
mumbles something about
no one understanding.

I think some people want to know everything
and some people
like me
would rather know only the smallest bit, the safest things, the
prettiest parts.

I want my mom to be
the version of my mother who is really good at
bridge
and making coffee cake and doing

eye makeup.

I do not particularly want this one
here
who has secrets and
worries
and feelings that are too big for a little yellow kitchen
in a little yellow house
on my sixteenth birthday.

"Everything will be okay," I mumble
before I head out to school, and I
consider
putting a hand on her back or
shoulder
like she used to do for me when I was upset by the world
but I
don't.
We don't
touch like that
anymore.

Mimi, 2022

Are our sixteenth birthdays this way
because of our mothers
and their sixteenth birthdays,
a sort of generational
curse
or tradition more powerful than
the notebooks?

I can't decide if it makes me feel less lonely or
somehow
more.
I guess
maybe
it's nice to be a part of something,
even if that
something
is misery.

I go back further
to someone I've never met,
only seen in the photographs on the wall in black-and-white:
Wendy's mother,
the one who had
secrets and a hazy way of talking about them,
my great-grandmother,

Betty.

In photos of her at sixteen she looks

sweet,
with the smallest nose and
a mint-green dress
with
tiny
pearl
buttons
down
the
front.

Betty, 1954
Sixteen

I am called lucky
like an accusation,
a thing I haven't yet earned

and probably never will
(my mother says, "I would have done anything to have what you
have")

lucky

for the pearl buttons she sewed on my dress
("my mother could never have afforded—")

lucky
for a table at Giorgio's
on my sixteenth birthday
("my sixteenth birthday was in the basement and Clarence
was—")

lucky
for Helen
my best friend with soft hair
and rich parents
("my best friend when I was sixteen was—well, let's just say she's
gone now")

lucky
for Peter

who brings a silver necklace and
a bundle of balloons and
That Smile

"lucky," Peter says
and he is looking
at the place
on me
where the heart charm hangs

    that place

                  there

(a place that doesn't feel lucky at all
his hand   there
then sliding

              here

where he isn't meant to touch

and later
Peter's thumb
a compass
for the things I wanted to keep

                  for myself)

("when I was sixteen boys wouldn't even look my way," my
mother says. "You're lucky you have that boy")

Betty, 1954
Sixteen, Part 2

"I'm sixteen"
"Me too."
"I haven't done this."
"Me too."
"I don't want—"
"Sure you do."

        we are in his car and it is   hot
        I am in his arms and they are   strong
        my parents are yards away inside the house and
        they are naive
            they are eating cake
                they are all wrong about Peter

"My dress."
"Who cares."
"The buttons."
"Buttons?"
"I can't lose them. They're pearl."
"Pearl, Betty?"
"They were my mother's."
"Your mother's pearl buttons."
"They were her mother's before."
"So your grandmother's pearl buttons."

        his hand is still   here
        and also

there

"You really want to talk about your grandmother's pearl buttons right now?"

I don't know how to say that
yes
that is all I really
want
to
talk
about.

One comes loose
pops off
stops him
us
it
from happening

"Next time no pearls, Betty. No grandmothers."

(I taste the idea of next time like
a promise that is too rich, too
shockingly sweet,

like birthday cake served
on a girl's sixteenth birthday
when she wonders if she is too old
for frosting roses,
candles,
and the person she's been until

just
right
now.)

Betty, 1954
Sixteen and a Week

I don't wear buttons
to the prom—
my dress yellow
and ruffled
and easy to reach
under
to pull
down
to tear
off

which Peter does
as he promised   (I suppose?)
he would.

No one ever keeps
the promises
you want them to keep.

(*I promise to love you forever,*
he'd said,
hot breath,
moments before.
This
I liked
more than the grabbing and touching and
the rest of it. I liked
forever

from the mouth of this boy who everyone
loves
who I must love
too
because we are here doing this and he is
Peter
and I am
lucky
he even looks at me.
That's what they all
say
at least.)

But I'm not so sure Peter knows much
about forever.

Betty, 1954
Sixteen and a Week, Part 2

It was
a hot night
and it was
a quiet corner
and it was
not the sort of thing anyone told me about.

Peter's hands were too big for his body,
like a puppy growing into its paws,
and his mouth was always
the tiniest bit
wet

and then it was over

but also never quite ended.

Betty, 1954

Helen tries a hundred ways
to ask me what I've let Peter do to me.

I don't tell her.
Helen doesn't do
that
exactly. She does
other things but not
that.

Helen and Peter went to the movies together
once or twice
and Helen was
good
that's what she said,
That's what everyone says about Helen
who knows all the words to all the hymns at church
and knows all the ways to be good
and all the ways to say
no.

She takes me to church
on Sunday—
dresses me in something white and pink
and high-necked and helps me work on my
smile.

I didn't know my smile needed
so much work.

I keep thinking about my yellow dress
with ruffles
and no
pearl
buttons.
A hundred pink-and-white dresses
can't erase the memory
of
that
other
dress.

"You should really make church a bigger part of your life,"
Helen says.
"God is watching," Helen says.
"We have to be stronger than boys. On the inside, I mean. We
have to keep them on the right path," Helen says.
"You have a goodness inside of you," Helen says.
"You can't let them have everything," Helen says. "Not if you
want them to
love you."

I almost tell her
but don't
that Peter said he loved me so maybe she's
wrong,

I get sleepy, listening to the minister,
and Helen
notices.
She jabs me in the ribs;
her face looks sharper than usual.
"This is for you," she says, nodding her chin
at the man in the robe mumbling about God.

I try to sing along with the songs,
but even that I do
all wrong.
"Quieter," Helen says. "Sweeter."
Until this moment, I have always loved
singing.

It is easier
I think
to be good
when you look like Helen, who is all
straight lines and nice smiles and perfect skin.

My body is so
loud.
If Helen could
she would tell my body to be
quieter
and sweeter
too.

On our way out the door, Helen puts her hand
on my shoulder
and somehow
that touch feels even worse
than all the other
touches
I didn't
exactly
say yes
to.

"People are talking," Helen says.
"About God?"

"About you."
"And Peter?"
"Mostly you."
"Well, tell them to stop."
"I'm trying to help."
"Try to help Peter."
"It's your job to help Peter do right. Peter is—he's wonderful,
isn't he? So you need to
help him
or else
let him go and be with someone who can be
good for him."
We both know that Helen still
holds a torch
for Peter.
So I say nothing
and wonder if he still holds a torch
too.

Helen and I used to go to piano class together
I hit the keys too hard
and she didn't hit them hard
enough.
We used to play with our dolls:
feed them air,
sing them lullabies,
read them books.

I'm not so sure
what happened
between putting our baby dolls to bed
in cardboard boxes
wrapped in table linens and pillowcases
and how things are

now

but we were the
same
almost
and now we are
somehow
not.

(Except: I still feel like a girl
who hits piano keys too hard
and kisses a plastic baby head
like it is something real,
but Helen keeps telling me I look
too—something—maybe too much
like
Marilyn Monroe,
her name said as a
whisper,
as if blonde hair and breasts and hips
and an airy little voice are
simply too—something—
for Helen's perfect
shell-shaped
ears.)

Betty, 1954

The thing is,
I don't look like Marilyn Monroe

at all.

Betty, 1954

Mom keeps telling me to wear something
else
for dinner at the club.

"Don't you have anything . . .
. . .
. . .
. . .
sweeter?" she says. "Those dresses from Helen,
maybe?"

I am tired
of wearing Helen's dresses,
with their frills,
the ruffles that
unshape me,
the lacy layers that
make my mother
sigh
in relief.

"Oh," she says when I walk down
in the pink-and-white
dress that I hate. "Oh yes, that's—
that's so much better, Betty. So much more
appropriate."

Her own dress

h
a
n
g
s

a size too big and
thicker than anyone needs
in May.

At dinner she eats
small bites of iceberg lettuce
and splits a steak with me.
I would have eaten
the whole thing
if she'd let me.

It seems silly
to wear pink
and eat half a steak
when I know
what
I did.

(What we did?
What Peter did, that I didn't stop?
Isn't it all
the same?)

Betty, 1954

The first few times Peter mentions
marriage,
we talk about
white dresses and flowers and rings engraved with words he's
whispered to me.

We talk about the color of my eyes and how they are sky or
ocean or both
maybe
because, he says, I am everything.
I am the sky and the ocean
and maybe something else,
too,
but he doesn't know
what.

We talk about love and how it is forever
and bodies that fit together
and building houses on lakes and his mother teaching me how
to make
pot roast
and his favorite
pie.

He tells me he wants to get married soon
like his father did,
young,
and his brother, too, eighteen and already living in a small home
outside his parents' place

with a skinny wife who puts flowers in vases,
arranges them
into tiny floral symphonies.

"I love that," Peter says.
"She sets the table, folds napkins into these perfect triangles.
When he gets up in the morning, she brings him coffee.
Before he even asks."

His eyes are misty, like the sky, I guess;
like sky or ocean
or just like how eyes get when they know what they want.

He wants me,
I think with a fast breath
that hurts a little.
Or
he wants his brother's skinny wife, but in my body,
and I guess I try to stop
thinking
that.

I want
Peter
or at least I want the way people look at me
when they see me with Peter.
Like they are seeing something
new
about me that they never noticed before,
like maybe I am more
good
worthy
beautiful
special

than they thought.

"You don't drink coffee," I say
instead of saying
*yes yes, I'll do all of those things, I will wait on you and make
your mornings
perfect.*

We are in his car
again and
                again
                        and again
and my skirt is still on
but nothing beneath.
My cardigan's unbuttoned, my hair starting to loosen,
which is what happens
after.

"I would start drinking coffee," Peter says. "If you made it
for me."
"*I* drink coffee," I say.
I have sips of my father's in the morning
while he looks at the paper,
and Dad smiles at each
sip,
a thing we share:
black coffee and the paper and the not-cooking of breakfast.

Peter doesn't reply,
doesn't ask how I take it
or why I like it
or who I drink it with—

he does not offer to be the one
to make the coffee
and bring it to me in bed
in the mornings
when we are married.

(Maybe I don't deserve
coffee in bed.)

(Maybe this is the absolute
best
I can hope for:
bare legs and wishing for
underwear,
saying a sort-of yes
in the back of the car
and waiting for him to tell me
today's
I love you.)

(Maybe I would like making coffee and
arranging flowers
and being a wife,
even though, if I'm honest, it sounds a little

dull.)

"I can work for my father," Peter says.
"I'll buy you a ring," Peter says.
"Maybe at Christmas," Peter says.
"I love you I love you I love you," Peter says.

But

"I love Helen," Peter says
later.

Mimi, 2022

My hand was a fist and it
u   n   f   u   r   l   s
reading Betty's pain.
Someone else's sadness
hurts
when it is all
laid bare
like that, and before I even
breathe
I button my own
cardigan all the way to the top,
like that might fix the
unbuttoned
past.

Betty's pearls are
here
in the box with Betty's diaries,
pearl buttons
like little promises of purity

or

not promises, no.

Little lies
about who we are
and what it means
and what they think we are telling them when we put on our

clothes
and brush our hair this way or

that.

The notebooks
are a little like that too, I think with a
shiver, a shrug, an uncertain breath. Filled with all these ideas of
who
we have to be, promises that it won't ever
change.
I mean,
eighty years
or whatever
is a long fucking time
for it to still be impossible
for a girl who looks like me
or Betty
to ever be wearing
the right thing. It is somehow never okay to have
this dress
and this body
at the same time.

Lately,
I make sure everything I wear
goes all the way to my
neck
and I write captions about how that's
sexier,
how it is cool to be
mysterious and modest. I write about learning how to sew
and how it liberates me from

wearing shit other girls wear
because I am not like other girls with their
bodies on display;
I am not like my mother in her headshots when she was my age,
all
pouty and
perky and
provocative.

Prairie Girl Chic,
someone wrote when I asked my followers,
what would you call my style?
Prude Who Wants It, another one
wrote.
Doing Your Best in an
Impossible Body, Mom wrote,
and I think it was meant to be
nice,
like the way she always nods
in sympathy at something bunching or gapping or fitting all
wrong.
"I know," she's always saying. "I got dealt the same
shit
hand."

But tonight,
alone
in my room,
I unbutton my cardigan
gently, like Betty might feel it across
time,
and I want to be gentle
with her,
with us.

I try on a
halter top, then a
black dress that I wanted to wear to the freshman formal,
then a tie-dyed
crop top, and I look and look and look and try to understand
where my body ends and I
begin.

I sew Betty's pearl buttons
to a green dress I made
that has pockets and cap sleeves,

except
I don't make buttonholes,
so they are
buttons that can't be
un-

buttoned.

And when Clinton texts
again and

again

about some party at some house on some street that's
pretty close to my street,
I do
finally

say
yes
but only because of those buttons
and the way they dot down my dress,
sewed on tight and leading

nowhere.

Mimi, 2022

"You look pretty," Clinton says
when he shows up at my door.
I want to say thank you, but I keep thinking about
Peter
and what he might have said to Betty to make her feel
safe
and how she
wasn't
and how that probably means I'm
not
or none of us ever really are,
so instead of thank you I say
"I sort of hate parties."
"No one likes parties," Clinton says. "We all just
go."
"Oh."
We stand there
looking at each other
in the truth of that tiny
oh until Clinton
s   m   i   l   e   s.

"Online you seem like you like parties.
It's kind of

nice

that you don't, actually. That you're

you." There he is, just
smiling
again.

"You don't know who I am or if it's nice
at all," I say.
"That's true," he says. "Now I just know you
don't like parties
and you lie online."
He winks
like it's not a flaw,
like it's a sort of sweet contradiction,
like it's a secret
we now share.

We are mostly quiet
except for the sounds of our footsteps as they   find
and then   lose
step with each other.
I think I like it best when we are
in sync,
our footsteps hitting the same gentle beats,
but I can't bring myself to whisper that sort of ridiculous
thought.

Finally, we get to a two-story house that smells like
scented candles
and shitty beer.
It's cold inside,
the place air-conditioned even in winter, and
Clinton gives me his sweater, which is blue and fuzzy
but the kind of fuzzy that also itches.
I am itchy
just generally. And I can't stop
looking around to determine who knows what about
my mom
and if they've decided that means something
about me
or if maybe
here
I can be a stranger
or at least be
that girl from online who you know everything and
nothing
about.

"Can I take a photo of this?" I ask Clinton,
as if his sweater is like
his baby or something
and maybe he doesn't want it
exposed online,
especially now when everyone's all over
my page.
"What will the caption be?" he asks. "Something about hating
parties?"
"Hating parties but loving sweaters," I say, and I try to decide if
my voice sounds
okay,
because my heart is sort of

not.
"Hating parties but liking the guy who belongs to this sweater?"
he asks.
"Okay, all right, calm down," I say,
but I'm laughing
and also saying in my head
over and over,
just be a person at a party,
just be a normal person at a party.
But it's actually
hard
to be a normal person at a party when the last party I went to
was three years ago
and was the
start of everything
or maybe the end,
I don't know, I can't keep track,
but I meant it
when I said I hate parties.
"I just want to post something not about
my mom
or whatever," I say. I say
my mom extra quiet, like if the words sound
small enough,
they might actually

                                           disappear.

I take the photo.
I caption it:
I'm not a party girl, I'm a sweater girl . . . especially if the sweater
belongs to a cute guy.
And right away
everyone comments that I'm

ignorant and callous and
cruel
for caring about cute guys
at a time like this
with everything her mother is going through
her mom must be so disappointed
she's being a
hero
and her daughter is vapid
is the next
what
Paris or Kim or other silly
girls who only care about makeup and boys
and their breasts, which clearly
she does
because look at her
in
that
sweater.

I almost show Clinton right then.
I almost
let him see me fall to pieces at how impossible it is to do
anything
right, because he seems like the kind of person who could
maybe
understand. But I just

can't.
I am
maybe
a notebook
that isn't quite sure
it wants to be read.

Still.
When he asks me to go outside to look at the moon I

                                                                        go

and when he says he wants to kiss me I

                                                                        do

and when he does, it feels
a little like the moon itself,
somehow warm and bright at once,
a familiar light in all
that
dark.

Mimi, 2022

I have a beer and turn off my
phone.
Here
at this party,
I have decided to forget.

I didn't want you, Mom said,
and I am here to forget
that
too.

"Is everyone here
trying to forget
something?" I ask Clinton. We are sitting
on a couch that is in the middle of
everything
and we're watching the party
u   n   f   u   r   l,
people's limbs getting looser,
voices louder,
people wobbling closer to one another,
hands on shoulders and then
around waists,
a girl in a sparkly skirt
suddenly making out with a girl
who never took off her jacket;
a few couples
pressed against the wall and others
twisted onto chairs that are meant for one body and not two.

"Even if they're not trying," Clinton says,
"they ultimately
will
forget,
right?"
I nod. We guess at who has had the most to drink
and who is eyeing who
and who is closest to throwing up
and who doesn't even want to be here at all.

I can't stop thinking about my mom's sixteenth birthday party in
the notebook,
so I laugh extra loud at whoever and whatever Clinton points
out,
and I drink the beer
faster
than I promised myself I would.

"The key is to people-watch, not actually participate," Clinton
says. "Then
tomorrow,
go online
and see what people have posted. It will be like
watching a movie get edited into something else.
No one will look
like that." He nods to
a group of guys who are red-faced and sweaty, hanging over each
other,
beer dribbling down their
chins.

I look at my lap.
I have been the edited selfie
and also

that other thing,
the messy thing, the photo no one was supposed to see.
Maybe it's the beer making my head
swim,
but probably it's
everything else.

Some girl—whose mother did not report her own decades-old
sexual assault without warning,
whose mother has always
wanted her,
some girl who has
probably
two parents and a sibling and maybe
for all I know
a horse and a bunch of friends and breasts that are the perfect
size—
flips her hair in this particular way
and smiles with her mouth closed at a cute guy
and touches his shoulder
sweetly.
So I flip my hair in that same way
and smile my quiet smile and touch
Clinton's shoulder
and I guess I am
trying to make the perfect selfie happen
now; I guess I want this moment
here
to have that perfect
sheen.

"Are you okay?" he asks,
like he already knows
I am being someone else.

I'm only good at pretending
online. In person I am
only really able to be me.

"Oh, no, I'm extremely fucked-up, actually," I say. "Like.
extremely. I thought you knew that." I smile in case he needs it
to be
a joke.

"Maybe you want to go home,
be with your mom?" he asks
instead of smiling back.

I stare at the girl across the room again,
like she might move in some way I can move
to look like a girl with a mom who is waiting up for her at
home.
But she's just sitting still, and I get distracted
by her shirt. It's
vintage, I think.
"What band is that? Like, Nirvana or something?" I ask Clinton.
"One of those
old bands no one actually listens to?"
"Nah, it's probably one of her homemade ones," Clinton says.
"She likes to make these
T-shirts, you know, usually ironic or
political or
whatever. It's—she thinks it's cooler than it is, but it's
a little cool. The clothes you post online are
cooler."

I squint at him to see if he means it.
I can't tell. The squinting makes him
blurrier. Everything's getting

blurrier.

"That does sound a little cool," I say, and
I turn to smile at Clinton, but he's
frowning at the girl.
I strain to see
whatever he's seeing,
and then
there it is
on her T-shirt,
newly made this afternoon, maybe,
a photo of my mother,
a puffy-paint crown on her head,
the word "ICON" printed beneath,
and when she turns,
on the back it says
"*Really* Believe Women."

I do not
become an armadillo. I become something else,
something that spins around fast and gets really
dizzy,
something that burns hot and shakes.

"I believe my mom," I say, quiet but hard.
"She's just one of those people who likes to push buttons—"
Clinton starts.
"I mean I believe her but she's also a really fucked-up—it's not
some, like,
fucking
easy thing that makes sense the way that girl's family
probably—"
"Hey, let's just go. She didn't know you'd be here or what you
and your mom's deal—"

"My mother is not some fucking
icon," I say. "I'm not some awful daughter. We aren't—she's my
mom
and it's—
I wish it was really simple so I could wear some perfect outfit
about it
too but unfortunately I haven't even spoken to her like at all—"
"I'll walk you home."
"I don't even know who she is
honestly
and neither does that girl
or anyone here
or you
but it's more complicated than some
fucking
homemade
piece-of-shit
shirt.
I mean. Fuck. Fuck that shirt. Hey! You! Fuck that shirt."
Clinton takes my hand and pulls
a little.
"Mimi. Come on. Let's go."
"I believe women who
believe
me!" I shout,
and a few people turn
but not that girl,
not the one who needs to hear it, so I try to say it louder, but
Clinton
gets me outside, so I'm really just saying it to
that stupid moon.

Mimi, 2022

"I'm sorry," Clinton says. "I know you didn't want to
think about
that."
"Whatever," I say, trying to let that
white-hot rage
pass through me so I can somehow be
a cute girl getting walked home
by a cute guy
and not this
huge mess who hates her mom.

"So you and your mom—"
"It's complicated."
"Online it seems like you guys are
best friends or whatever."
"It's the same as the people at the party. We look really good
in matching outfits
and baking cookies and, like,
laughing at nothing, but
the reality is—
I don't know.
Not
that."
Clinton nods. I nod back, and try to let that repetitive motion
calm me down,
calm all of me way
down.

"Were you guys ever close?" Clinton asks, and

the answer is yes,
but the yes hurts more than a no
because the yes means something
changed.
I shrug.

We keep walking and soon it starts
to snow.
"I love snow," I say, not to change the subject
really
but because it's so true I have to say it. I love it landing on my
lashes and dusting my
hair. I love that it looks like stars falling from the sky
and that it makes walking home feel like something
more.
In the snow, I am not the person who yelled at the stranger
about her shirt. In the snow I am someone
else.
"It would make a nice picture," I say. "I could post something
about,
like,
starting fresh? I could apologize to that girl? Do you know her
name?
I could
fix it all,
I think. If I could just figure out
exactly the right thing to say or
do,
I could fix

everything. You know?" I look up at Clinton,

feeling the snow on my lashes
and how it is heavier and wetter
than I want it to be.
Maybe
he knows
how to be. How to fix
the thing with the girl
and the thing with my mom
and the way the people online feel about me
and also
whatever else
about me
that needs

fixing. I look at him and wait
for those answers.

"The thing about snow," Clinton says, "is that it's really hard to
capture it
in a photo, you know. It's like
the moon:
it never looks the same and you end up being like,
no no, I swear it was
so cool,
but in the picture the moon is just this, like,
random-ass circle all far away
and snow is just
these white smudges
that look like a mistake."

It's true

what he's saying,
and the snow falls harder
and I want him to fix it and fix me because I just
don't know how
to fix any of it.
"A lot of things that look
like mistakes," he goes on,
"are actually
sort of beautiful, I think. Maybe,
I don't know,
maybe there aren't really
mistakes.
Maybe everything's
like the snow. You have to really look at it,
really stand in a flurry of it,
to understand what makes it
special."

He shrugs.
He's just sitting there shrugging even though he's said the most
beautiful thing I've ever heard
and I
kiss him
hard
in the snow
and I almost tell him everything—
all about why my mother and I started being
weird
and what it feels like to be home
alone when everyone's talking about you,
and I almost tell him
also
about Betty and Wendy and the impossible way history
can feel present,

can feel like right now,
especially when his hands brush
Betty's buttons,
trying to get underneath my dress,
which is maybe okay or isn't okay, but until I know for sure I
need to just
step away
and not say
any of it. Because if I say
any of it,
he might stop looking at me
like I am
a beautiful blizzard that has to be
experienced
to be
understood,
like I am
the way the snow is, too wet and too cold but also
what you wanted
somehow.

"Thanks for walking me home," I say
instead of saying everything else.
"Thanks for coming with me," he says.

He kisses me
this time
and the snow falls
harder. Beautiful and impossible to
capture.

Mimi, 2022

It is maybe three or four in the morning
when there is a

click
slam
crash
bang

and my first waking thought is
Betty!
because I was dreaming about her
and also because she
and the notebooks
and me
are the only ones in this house.

Then I hear Eric's voice:
"Easy, easy, chickadee"; and Mom's: "I'm fine, I'm

fine."

We only say that when we are not
fine.

It's strange

how the house feels

emptier

now that it's

full.

Mimi, 2022

When I wake again,
there is the sound of Mom snoring on the couch,
and Eric is in their bedroom,
and the notebooks
hum and haunt upstairs,
a sort of
white noise   whisper
that I can't seem to shake.

So I don't.

I walk from my room through the kitchen and living room,
where the TV is still on,
reruns of the news,
and they are talking about my mom:
"Walter Bruce says he never had a relationship with anyone
unwilling
or under the age of
consent,
and that in America
we all have to take responsibilities for our actions,
even if we're not
proud of them." Then there is a clip of Walter Bruce,
his voice hoarse and also kind of
over it:
"I'm not proud of everything I've done,
but that doesn't make it
illegal." He gives this sort of
sickening smile,
like he's already

won.

My knees sort of
waver,
like they're not sure they want to hold me
anymore,
but I tell them to
straighten,
strengthen,
keep it together,
even though it's
bullshit
that Walter Bruce is on TV in a
gray suit and my mom is
in a pile on the couch
in a sweat-stained T-shirt,
smelling like
yesterday,
like surrender,
like French fries and tequila and shame,
so maybe
he has
actually
already won.

I never see her this way,
never except once
when I told her what happened at the party
in early March three years ago.
She was like this for three days,
then told me
to
forget it
and that maybe I
misunderstood it,
and then we sat in the house

for all those quarantined months,
not
talking about what I could have possibly
misunderstood.

And maybe it felt okay that she didn't
believe me
or had to
stop believing me,
because it was better than watching her edges
crumble.
I liked her better
knitting and baking bread and
touching up the paint in the kitchen and the bathroom,
finding little odd jobs and new recipes all through the pandemic.
It was lonely but
safe.

And now she's
here again,
looking like she went to last night's rager,
looking like
the sorry underside of a social media
post.

I guess
this is what I do to her.
I guess this is why
she didn't want me
to begin with.

The ladder creaks and crackles when I climb up to the attic,
but Mom doesn't even move.

Maybe some small part of me
hoped she'd wake up
to join me here,
like some strange family reunion—
me and my
mom and our

ghosts.

Betty, 1954
Sixteen and a Month

Maybe it is the way
Helen says the word

                            No

that makes Peter listen.

Maybe it is the way Helen says the word

                            No

that makes Peter love her.

I try it now,
alone
in my room,
looking in the mirror
at the girl who is now
not
Peter's.
"No," I say.
But still
even now
it sounds

                      shaky

more of a

                      maybe-yes

than an

                      actual-no.

"No," I say again.
But I am probably smiling
or doing something with my hands that says
                      not-really-no

and besides
there is my body
all sloped and   what's the word my mother said
once

              supple

and isn't that its own version of

                            yes?

Betty, 1954
Sixteen and Two Months

Helen asks me to meet her at Harry's Diner
and Mom says I have to go
because it's the right thing to do
even though it is not right
for me.
"Betty. Hi. I ordered us
pancakes," Helen says. And she looks
sorry.
Not sorry for what she did
but sorry
for me.

The jukebox is playing
Doris Day's "Secret Love," which is
swoony and sweeping
and it's the sort of song that
once
would have made me think of me and Peter
but listening
now
it is so clearly about
Helen.
His secret love.
Who isn't a secret
anymore.

"I'm not very hungry," I say, which is almost true:
I'm hungry but
ill.

I'm hungry, but when I eat, my body
rejects it.
"Well, more for me, then," Helen says,
and maybe,
maybe Helen is awful?
Or maybe everyone is a little bit
awful?
I'm trying to reorganize the world
after Peter told me he wanted to be with Helen.
I don't know
what parts fit where anymore,
like maybe now the sky is an ocean
and pancakes are broccoli
and love is
a lie.

"I know you and he . . . but that was a silly thing, wasn't it?"
Helen says
now. "And Peter and I are—well—I wanted to be the one to tell
you."
She holds up
her left hand
and it is
heavy,
sparkling,
a bit of cruelty wrapped around her finger.

The ring
is big
and it
shines.

I nod

at the way

nothing makes sense and how that
in and of itself
makes a sort of strange sense.

"Silly," I repeat, trying out how it sounds. I suppose
it's
not wrong.
"We were a silly thing. I was silly."

(The heart charm he gave me is
still around my neck,
thoughts of Peter's mouth,
Peter's hands,
still banging around my heart—
the end of us is so dangerously
close
to the beginning
it is hard to tell
one
from
the
other.)

(It is both,
this particular Now.

An end
and

                                        a beginning.)

Betty, 1954
Sixteen and Two Months, Part 2

The half a pancake I ate with Helen
sits in my stomach
and I wait
and wait
and

wait

for the phone to ring.
And for it to be Peter
telling me
why
or
when
or

how.

The last time he said he loved me he looked
sad about it.
And maybe I should have known
then
that I am not the kind of girl that a boy like Peter
marries
even if I *am* the kind of girl he
sadly
loves.

"A watched pot never boils," my mother says
when it has been two hours
of me sitting in the stiff wooden chair
next to the phone.

"A phone isn't a pot," I say. "Peter isn't
water."

Except right now he feels like water—
essential,
the only thing I truly need
to survive.

Mom and Dad eat dinner.
It's a roast,
something I used to like but now smells
awful.

Somewhere, Helen is thinking about dresses and flowers
and Peter is thinking about Helen's sweet face
and how good she is
at praying
at buttoning her dresses all the way to the top,

at saying no,
at making banana bread,
at curling her hair.

"You were in young love," Mom calls out from the table. She
says it like
it was a thing that happened
years
ago, but
only two months have passed since the first time
and maybe six weeks
since the last time
and I need that to mean something, except Mom keeps talking
and says,
"It was nothing, this sort of thing
happens all the time. You will meet someone more

suited to you.
Peter is
a different—

well
we should have known
perhaps
that it wasn't meant to be, even though it would have been
wonderful."

Mom sighs
the sound of a dream dying.
the letting go

of what could have been.

I sigh too.

I don't know what it is that puts Helen and Peter
there
and me

                              all the way over here.

But I have some

guesses.

Betty, 1954
Sixteen and Four Months

My mother knows
before I do,

smelling something on my skin
or seeing something
around my belly.

"Oh. Betty. No," Mother says, looking at the
s   w   e   l   l.

It is true
the way truth is always bigger
than the things we want.

For a moment
I
light up.

"I have to tell
Peter," I say. "He'll—"

"Peter is engaged
to Helen," Mother says. "Peter's parents—
they won't—
we certainly can't—
Oh Betty."

"But maybe if he knew—"

Mother
sighs.
The dream dying
again.

"There's a place in New York," Mother says, "for girls like you."
Mother's voice is tight
like it has been
zipped
up.

(I do not ask
what kind of girl
I am
like.)

My father says nothing,
not now
and not ever
again.

Betty, 1954

I don't care about Helen's ring   (except of course I do).
A ring is different from
a baby.

And maybe this baby
will look like Peter
and maybe Peter will love the way the baby
stares up at him
and maybe that will
make him love me
too.

My mother keeps talking about
the place in New York,
but isn't there also a place
for me
right here?

And isn't that place
right exactly
where Peter's arm meets his shoulder?
Aren't I meant to be
tucked   right   there?

Isn't there a place for me
in one of those small houses
by the river,
with Peter working for his dad
and me learning how to make

mashed peas
or whatever else babies eat?

I'm not great at
much
really
but I think I could figure out
how to make
mashed peas.

I know I could figure out
how to love a baby
our baby
my baby. I think I am
figuring out how to love it
already.

I walk to Peter's house,
which is only a street away,
but it could be miles
for how slowly I move.

His mother answers the door
like she knows,
her eyes all over my
body.
"Hello, Betty," she says. "We weren't
expecting you."

I ask for Peter and she   hesitates,
bites her lip once,
and,
I think,
tries to come up with a reason to say no.

She used to like me   I think.
    She used to at least
                                        tell me if I had a
                                        smudge of something
                                        on my face
                                        and ask me about my
                                        parents' health.

No longer, I suppose.

"Only for a moment, please, Betty," she says at last.
"Peter has a lot to do,
and Helen is coming over later to talk about
the wedding."

I don't know if Helen is coming   or not,
    but she smiles at   saying it.
    She's happy to   remind me

who I am,

who I have always been
and will
always
be.

And I know
now
why Mother keeps talking about a faraway home.
Why no one is planning our
wedding.

It is this look
here,

the one on Peter's mother's face:

unblinking and
waiting to
dismiss me.

Betty, 1954

"It's not what we imagined. Being young parents. Struggling.
Like that."
He doesn't look at my   belly after I tell him
what's growing   there.
"Well, no," I say.   I tell my voice to
          still.   Please.
               But it   can't.

"It's not what we imagined, but it's
what is happening," I say.
I try to make my voice as
soft
as Helen's
is sweet.
Peter trills his lips,
blows air through them
so they make a sound of
mild
irritation.

"I'm so young," he tells
the floorboards.
He's young
to get married to Helen, too,
but I don't say that.
I don't want to remind either of us

of that.

"I'm young," I say.
"Exactly."
"I'm sixteen," I say.
"Exactly," Peter says.
"So."
"So."
"When this happens, people get married," I say.
It's what my mother
should have said
but didn't.
I know I am going to cry by the
tightening of my
throat
and the way my stomach
turns;
my head goes all
light.
"You said you wanted to marry me
someday."

And it is only right
then
that I realize someday isn't a
promise;
it's not a real date in time.
Someday
is just an idea we dream up,
and dreams
die
fast.

"My parents—" he says.
"My brother—" he says.
"I want to—"
"I need to—"
"My life is—"
"What we had was—"
"Betty. You are so great but you are not the kind of girl
I can marry. You know that. And
I mean
we haven't
in a long time.
That baby is
not
mine."

Maybe
for Peter
there were other girls in other cars
with other kinds of pearl-buttoned dresses.
But for me
there was only him
and still
somehow
I'm the one who looks

bad.
"Of course this is your baby," I say. "I've only ever—"
"Come on,
Betty."

I reach   for his hand

to put it on my

belly.

Once it is there
he'll know
the way I know
that this is our future
and that it is
beautiful
and thumping and
ours.

But he
jerks his hand away.

Sometimes I hope for   impossible things.

Like love.

"I love Helen She said she told you. About our—that we plan
to—I thought she told you."
"She did," I say. "But this baby is—"

"Not mine," Peter says. "The baby is
not mine. I'm engaged to Helen and you are
trying to mess that up. You are
trying to drag me into something
because of who I am

and who
you are."

I should go home.
A different girl would go home.
Maybe Helen
would go home.

I cannot.
I stay and remind him about the best, longest afternoons we
had,
not that long ago,
really.

There was

                              the dock,
                                 the mosquitoes,
          the way my lips felt sticky and red after all those berries,
                                 as if red is a feeling.
               (But isn't it? Wasn't I red then? Aren't I blue now?)

"That was all a long time ago," Peter says.
He says nothing
of berries and docks
or what color
his feelings   are.

                                        Helen-colored,
                                        I guess.
                                        Taupe and beige
                                        and
                                        tan.

    Peter's mother

appears
and I can see from her face she has
listened. She has
heard.

"It's time for you to go," she says. "Peter
doesn't have time
for this silliness.
This has
nothing to do with us.
So please
leave us be. There are places
for girls like you. Surely your mother
will know what to do."

"I'm sorry," Peter says in a voice I
finally
recognize
as the one he used with me. Sweet and simple and
real. Like maybe he really is
sorry.

But his mother grabs his arm and
squeezes.
I think it must be
hard
because he
winces.

I almost ask
about boys like Peter
and what places are meant for
them.

But instead
I leave
before they can finish telling me
where
I
belong.

Mimi, 2022

You'll probably end up with a
nice girl,

I text Clinton.

Probably, he texts back
and I wonder what it feels like to know
something about
what you
deserve. *But aren't you*
a nice girl?

I type out answers that I then
delete.

I scroll through my profile
and all the photos there
to look for the answer.

I am in his sweater.
I am in the "Believe Women" T-shirt.
I am wrapped up in a blanket that someone paid me to wrap
myself in.
I am in a bathing suit but it's
a one-piece that doesn't show
cleavage.
I am in high-waisted jeans and a billowy peasant shirt
that I made from old clothes we were going to throw away,
and my hair is mermaid-wavy and my eyes are
sad.

I am in a flannel shirt two sizes too big, but my eyes are
lined in black and my hair is
bedroom-messy, according to the comments.
I am in a hoodie and a tank top underneath,
and my hair's in a ponytail, but they say that's
sexy,
they say it's unzipped just the perfect
amount,
but I had only wanted them to see
that I'd made the tank top myself
and added embroidery to the hoodie,
but they don't, they only see
the zipper,
I guess.
I am in a dress that matches Mom's, and they are both
pink and hitting an awkward part of our
legs
and buttoned up to our necks
because I made them that way so that people would notice
the color, the fabric, the delicate lines, and not
us beneath them,
but the dresses are
tight,
I guess,
because everything is too tight
and all kinds of wrong
when the world isn't built for bodies like mine
and hers
and Betty's.

Even the clothes I make myself
don't
fit
aren't

right
somehow still
don't belong to
me.

So I don't know,
I guess maybe I am
trying to be the kind of nice girl
that Clinton might end up with
or just be with
for a blissful bit,
but

it won't work,
according to the evidence.

Betty found out
about what kind of girl she was allowed to be
and it was,
like me,
not the kind of girl who nice boys want to be with and not the
kind of girl
who gets a sweet
happily ever after.
I bet Betty's mom
didn't believe her either
when she told her what Peter said and did and what she
did and did not
want.

Or no,
Betty
probably never told her mom

much of anything,
and maybe that's the lesson
here.

Mimi, 2022

The phone keeps
ringing
and Mom
somehow
keeps sleeping
and the people on TV keep showing that one photo of her
looking beautiful and nervous
or maybe beautiful and excited
or maybe beautiful and scared
or maybe beautiful and seductive.

A panel of people discuss which she is,
all of them only agreeing on
her beauty and that her beauty means

something.

I think it means
something
too.

It means she should have been more careful,
or maybe not there at all. It means she should have worn the
clothes
I wear,
which cover up the things that make people want you. It means
she should not have worn that shirt, with its

deep V. Shirts like that are for
other girls with other bodies that are not
these bodies, the kind you have to be
careful
with.

(I have worn that kind of shirt
but it's been three years
and she is the one who told me to
stop.)

I have seen the way she is
around guys,
how she likes to swing her hips and dip her head back when she
laughs.
I wonder if she was
like that
with him, with Walter Bruce,
and what it means
if she was.

(It was a long time ago,
though,
and the Mom in that photo
they're all discussing,
she looks

like me.
Like me three years ago,
before I knew
how to dress or

why. I feel bad for
the Mom they are discussing,
Tiffany,
but it's harder to feel bad
or feel
anything
for this one here
on the couch.)

(And also. Also.
The shirt looks
good on her. I
like the color and cut and
for a moment
I want to wear it too.
But it's not
allowed. She
and those boys at that party
and everyone at every party
and all the people online
have made that
clear.)

"You're back," I say when
finally
she gets up.
She nods.
She does not apologize for what she said on the phone,
which was a dozen tiny awful things and one huge one
folded in,
said so quickly I might have missed it,

I wish I'd missed it,
but I didn't:
I didn't even want you.
"I wish you'd told me you were going to—"
"I did it for you. For all girls."
"But you didn't even tell me."
"It's complicated, Mimi. It was—you watch the news, you
know. The story was
going so fast
and I had to
act."
"But what about me?" I say in this voice that must be left over
from when I was seven and not getting to eat ice cream for
breakfast or
ten and not getting a cell phone for my birthday or
thirteen and
coming home from a party
that I wasn't supposed to go to
and wished I hadn't
gone to after all.

"I'm trying to do something important," she says, and her voice
sounds young,
too,
like the one from her notebooks
that I am not ready to hear.

"I tried to do the right thing," I say, which is,
I think,
true. "I tried to say what you would have wanted me to
say."
Eric plods downstairs,
always at the most important part
of the most important conversations,

to tell me I'm wrong
and Mom's right
and that's it.
He does it now:
"Your mom is a brave woman to tell her story
and you undermining her on your
ridiculous account isn't helping anything."
"You weren't here," I say, finally letting something

u
n
s
p
o
o
l

inside of me.

"You didn't even
take my calls,
Mom. You didn't even—
you never—
you left me
here."

There is this moment,
this

glorious,
heart-stopping moment,

where I am sure she has heard me
and it has mattered

and she will turn to me, her face
alight
with love and understanding,
and I lean in to the
hope
of that.

But
no.
It's not
that.

"You're sixteen, Mimi," she says
instead.
Like that means
I should be all done with my needing
of her.

          ("You're thirteen,"
          she said,
          back when I told her I didn't know
          that drunk girls should expect
          their photos to be taken,
          their bodies to be
          talked about. *"Thirteen,"* she'd
          repeated
          when I asked if she would
          do something
          to fix it.)

So
okay
I guess
I'll try

again
to be
done
with the needing of

anyone.

Mimi, 2022

An hour later Mom is
upright
at the kitchen table
on the phone
answering questions
when and how and where and why

they already know the

who.

She is
Professional Mom
right now,
in glasses and a crisp shirt. Mom has always been a little like
Barbie,
shifting into different outfits and hairstyles
depending on what she's doing or,
let's be honest,
who she's
dating.
"I was an actress," she says
when I ask her why she plays these
parts,
why she can't just be
Regular Standard-Issue Mom
all the time.

I sit outside the kitchen and listen in—
It was
once
and no I most certainly was not
drinking
I didn't drink

then.

He talked about my lips
and my

heart
but he was looking at my

breasts
and rubbing my

thigh
and I was so young I didn't know
what to do,
so I let him get closer
because of course it was a work meeting and
then it happened so fast
not sex
no
it's still illegal even if it's not
sex

right?
I know I said no
but probably not
enough
or maybe he didn't hear
but
I didn't want it
and it was obvious and so
yes
it happened
just that way.
Has anyone else
stepped forward? Is there
anyone else?

Mom's voice sounds
at the end there
the way it does when she asks Eric
if he thinks they'll get married someday,
the way it sounds when she
asks if she looks okay
in photos online,
if people are saying anything
nice.

It is a sound that
deflates me,
her desperate
wanting.

I thought maybe
we'd stop wanting
so badly
someday.

I try to sort through the rest of the words
about saying no
and not
sex
and thighs and
lips
but my brain only wants to linger
on her asking if there are other girls
with her same story.

Are there other girls with mine?
my mind whispers before I tell it to
be quiet.
Questions like that make me
shiver. They are too

real.

Upstairs
there are probably
answers
but maybe I don't want answers,
so when she hangs up I mumble something about going out.

"Where?" she asks
"Just out," I say.
"It's some guy,
isn't it?" she asks.

"Mom." I don't say yes or no. I guess in some part of my brain
I thought maybe I'd text Clinton
just to see
if he was around.
"Don't do this to me," she says.
"I'm not doing anything to you," I say. "I barely
know you."
I think maybe it will hit too hard but actually
I'm not even sure she hears or

cares.

"You need to be
better," she says. "We have a responsibility now
to get this man locked up and you need to
shut down your accounts and
make sure your classmates don't say anything
about you that would make me
look bad
and you do not need to be
cavorting
with some
asshole teenager
who just wants to
feel you up."

"He doesn't want—"
"Of course he does. Look at you. That's what they all
want."
Her eyes are

wanting to cry,
remembering,
I guess,
what it was to be my age,
but we are not the same,
and I almost scream it at her
WE ARE NOT THE SAME
but I don't
because,
well,
we are,
aren't we?

There it goes again,
the shiver
from asking questions
too
scary
to answer.

"What about Eric?" I ask, even though the question is
gross
and this conversation is
awful
and the door is   right   there
    and I should really just   walk on through it.

"Eric is saving this family," Mom says.
I think my heart
sighs;
all of me
sighs
and sort of
screams? But also stays

silent.

"Saving the family?" I ask, but I don't want the answer and my voice
breaks
on the words.

I am
cracking open,
breaking down
because of Betty and Clinton and
snow and
the things my mother keeps saying that I want to not hurt but
still just really

do.

I keep my eyes on the door. If I keep them there, they won't
cry.

"You are the one
causing all the
problems," Mom says. She says it
right to me,
like she wants to make sure I hear it.
"Once again." That part is
quieter,
under her breath,
but still something I am meant to
hear.

The phone's ringing again.
Another interviewer or lawyer,
I don't know.
My heart is
beat beat beating,
so I open the door to get away
from the things she keeps saying to let me know I am
unwanted and bad and wrong—

and outside there is a
swarm
of people taking photographs and asking questions
about my mother the hero and how it feels to be her daughter
and I should definitely say
nothing
but my mouth says,
"I don't know anything about who my mother was or
is
really, so leave me
alone. This is her
thing. I'm not a
part of it. No one ever even told me
anything about
any of it."

The instant the words are out of my mouth
I hate them
and myself for saying them,
but it's too late:
they are tapping on their phones and snapping more photos
and I have done a bad thing. Of course I have.
Because I *am* the bad thing.

The truth of it
hits me hard and I close my eyes and try to speak
again,
better this time.
"I mean, she's my mom," I say,
trying to
be good, "and I love her and
believe her
and that's it."
I am blushing and shaky and they write this down,
too,
take photos of it.
I shrink
from the flashes,
my arms moving in and my head

down.

"No comment," I try,
a third attempt,
way too late,
but it's what people say in movies,
rich people who know what they're doing, so I say it and
lower my head even farther
and move through them
and
somehow
somehow
somehow am thinking
how glad I am
that I am wearing
boots with three-inch heels

and a sweater two sizes too big
so that none of them will write anything about my
tiny
curvy
suspicious
body.

But also I am thinking:

fuck.

Mimi, 2022

I messed up, I text Clinton.
I mess up all the time, he says.
This was
worse, I text, because it surely, surely was.
Meet me at Northside and
tell me about it, he says.

I don't exactly want him to see
the worst part of me
but also
I have nowhere else to go.

And also

the worst part of me

is

maybe

the only part there is.

Mimi, 2022

"Well, anyway, Merry Christmas Eve," he says when I get there,
and I
squint.
"Is it?" I ask.
"Sure is."

He has already bought me a hot chocolate,
which I didn't ask for but maybe I wanted,
I don't know,
who doesn't want hot chocolate?

It's a little bitter,
the kind they make here,
but creamy. I don't say
thank you.

He leans in to kiss me but he
stops
before he gets to my lips.
"You look sad," he says.
I try to remember the last time someone noticed something
about me
that was not
what I was wearing
or what it did to my
body
or whether they
approved.
It's been,

I don't know,
a while.
A
really
long
while.

He leans back. I guess he doesn't kiss
sad girls
and that's probably good but also
when I'm sad
I sort of want to be
kissed
maybe.
"You can tell me stuff," he says when I have said
exactly nothing.
I keep looking around for more
reporters,
more people with cameras who will capture this moment where
my body leans toward him
or this one where I frown, thinking about my mother
or this one now where I bury my head
in my hands
for the things I have said
and the impossible ways I have ruined everything.
I am having trouble deciding
who I hate the most:
Eric
my mom
Walter Bruce
the reporters

or me.

I start some sentences in my head but they're all
wrong.
They all sound like some idea of what a person says
in a moment like this and they keep getting crowded out
by the insistent Christmas music Jake is playing
over the speakers.
"You're catching me in a moment—
my family in this moment—
and it's not a moment I
understand.
There's a lot I don't know.
And some of it I thought I did. But now
it sort of feels like things were this one way and I'd figured out
how to
be
in that
and lately everyone's decided that things are going to be a whole
different way
and no one asked me.
No one asked me any of this—
what I wanted to look like,
for one,
or who my mother would be,
or what she might say to change the world,
and how I have to live in that changed world
too.
People don't ask
girls
what they want
sometimes, you know?"

(I am thinking of Betty and also
me. Now and when I was thirteen
and also
always. And maybe I'm thinking of
Mom,
too,
in some trailer,
all made up and coiffed,
living her dream that was actually,
just like everything else
they offer us,
not very dreamy
at all.)

I'm breathless.
It's a lot of talking
for someone who hasn't had friends in a while.
And my heart is still
quick and shaky from earlier
and I'm
trying to take a perfect picture of my hand holding hot
chocolate because that will make me feel
okay. That has to make things
okay. I take
five photos, but they are all blurry and lopsided and
wrong.

Before I can take a sixth, Clinton grabs my hand.
It's
nice.

"You don't say any of that
online," he says.

It doesn't sound like a judgment or even a question;
it just
is.
So I just
nod.
"I don't know much either," he says, and it's a sort of nothing
thing to say,
except it's also everything. And maybe we were going to kiss
or something,
but my phone starts lighting up
and it's Mom
and she's pissed,
and I can't stay in Northside drinking hot chocolate,
wondering if I can get one more kiss before he finds out how
awful I am
forever.

So I walk home in the cold,
looking out for patches of ice,
loving how—
here on the road,
in tall boots and a loose sweater and a coat I made from
someone's old blazer and someone else's
ski parka
and a hat over my hair
so no one knows if it is bedroom-messy or not—

I know what to watch out for.
I know how to stay
safe.

Mimi, 2022

Eric meets me outside the house. He is

grim.

"What you said to those reporters—" he starts.
"I know."
"You are so out of line, you are so . . ." He searches for a word
and I'm
terrified
to find out which one he'll land on.
". . . troubled," he finishes. "And ungrateful. You don't know
all your mom does
for you."

I close my eyes for one
moment
and picture myself back at Northside,
drinking hot chocolate
in a cute sweater
with a cute boy,
and I try to nestle into that reality
instead of this one
here.

I try to imagine
this

                                      faraway

day
where I am just

sweaters and hot chocolate and tiny kisses that turn into longer
kisses
and maybe I'm in a big city working for some
cool designer who
listens to me who
likes me
who doesn't know anything about
Tiffany Dovewick or Walter Bruce or
me
really
even.

"I'm talking to you, Mimi," Eric says, all
loud
and fast, and the dream just sort of

d
r
o
o
p
s.

"I tried to fix it," I said. "And it's not like I said it
didn't happen
or something, I just said—"

"You're her daughter. You saying you never heard anything about
it—
saying you don't know
who she is. God, Mimi. *God.*"

The only other time Eric and I have really had it out

was when I was thirteen
and quarantine was starting
but he hadn't shut down the bar yet
and someone there was talking about
the photo of me from the party
and girls today
and how
stupid we are
and Eric came home and told me he was
so embarrassed
like it was something wrong that I
did
and not something wrong that was done
to me.

"I can talk to the reporters again," I say, looking around for
them
now.
"I got them to leave," he says. "We won't be letting that happen
again. And you are
grounded,
of course,
and maybe more. Probably more. What you've done—
your mother can't look at you. Doesn't want to speak with you
now,
or for a while."

I close my eyes again
and I am
@MimiDove and I am thirteen and making
homemade pasta with my mother and we are in
matching aprons and everyone says we are
adorable.
Outside the photo that is online we

fought about flour and what to wear and
it was a
pandemic
and the house felt small and sad and scary.
But in the photo
we threw our heads back when we laughed and we had
flour on our noses
and we sang
Italian opera while we rolled out the pasta
and cut it into strips.
It's weird
how something can feel so
close,
so
gettable,
and also so
impossible.
A photograph of a thing that happened

sort of.

"You don't even get it, do you?" Eric says. "You just
sit around daydreaming and
photographing and thinking the world revolves around you and
your
weird clothes and teen drama." He shakes his head.
Eric just
says things
so direct and terrible,
so
cutting. And I am
lost in all of it. I can't even
reply

really
to his hunched shoulders and heavy
brow. But I
try.

"I think about
everything," I say. "I think about it
when you and Mom are gone and leaving me alone with
nothing to do
but think about it." I don't
look at him when I talk. If I
look at him,
I'll go quiet, the way I always do.
"It's not like I said she was
lying. I told
the truth,
which is that
I didn't know and no one
included me in any of this."

Eric shakes his head and shakes it
some more.

Eric took Mom and me to an art museum
once
when he was trying to impress her or maybe even me,
back when he was new and I felt
hopeful
just at the idea of my family looking
like everyone else's.
I had never been to an art museum before. It's not the sort of
thing
Mom ever thought to do. We wandered these echoey white
rooms and

some people had audio guides telling them what to think and
feel
but I was so happy to be free.
Mom and Eric held hands and wandered ahead of me
when I decided to stay in this room of abstract
pieces.
I got lost in some of those paintings—
all the colors and shapes and blank spaces and me
standing there
trying to find meaning in all of it.

Only a few weeks later Eric stopped trying to impress me
and we never went to the art museum again. He never invited
me
anywhere
with them again,
actually.

But. I'm thinking of those abstract paintings and the way I got
lost in looking at them.
This moment with Eric
feels like the underside of that—there's all these shapes and
words and
feelings and decisions and accusations coming at me
and I'm just standing here
trying to pick out the heart of it all;
trying to make meaning
of the mess
the way I tried
years ago
to make meaning from strange, abstract beauty.

I can't go to the museum to stare at complicated,
unknowable

images
now
but I can go to the attic
to stare at complicated,
unknowable
other lives. And maybe if I sit there for long enough
I'll understand.

(There was one painting
at the museum. It was
all these different shades of blue
swimming across the canvas
and I stared at it for
ages
until I was pretty sure
I understood something about
calm and color and why everything
is always
a little bit
blue,
including me.)

(Maybe the journals,
if I stare long enough and read
everything,
will be like that blue painting
someday.)

(On the way up to the attic I catch sight of Mom on the couch.
The TV is
loud
and her name is mentioned
and someone says that she might not be

reliable,
that she never even told
her own daughter,
and she hangs her head
and approximately 500 things are true
at once
in that moment.)

(I think of the painting again,
all of those shades,
each one of them still
somehow
blue.)

(I open her notebook as soon as I get to the attic
in the hopes of visiting
some other version of her,
some other
shade
of blue.)

Tiffany, 1999

I have an audition
and Mom drives me
but she sighs at every
light,
rolls her eyes at every
turn.

Dad is the one who likes going with me,
but he's been working late,
so it's Mom and me
and everything she wishes I wasn't.

I turn the music up and she turns it
back down
like she has something
important
to say.
"My grandmother was one too," she says, finally. It sounds like
she's been working on this sentence
for quite
some time. "Grandma Virginia.
Before she was a mother, of course."
> Sometimes Mom speaks like words are rocks.
> Sometimes Mom says the word *mother* like it is a curse
> placed on women.

"One what?" I ask.
> one bad girl
> one slut

one disappointment
one person she has given up on

"An actress." it is another word that is a rock
"Silent films."
"That's so cool!" I say,
and take it as a sign
that I will be cast
as Girl Number Three
in the cereal commercial,
fulfilling my actress legacy.

Mom shakes her head like it is not cool
at all.

"I read about her
when I was your age. I read her
notebook." Mom is speaking
carefully, and I don't know why. The notebooks are
this
thing we have, the way Rachel's family has china that brides get
at their weddings
and Tyler's family displays
trophies they've all won at sports things.

"Oh. Cool. I'll check that out."
Mom shakes her head.
"It's not like that," she says. "It's not for fun."
"Right. Okay. Not for fun."
"You have to take something seriously, Tiffany."
"I'm serious." I make a silly face. Wag my tongue and wiggle my
fingers by my ears.
Mom used to like when I was a little bit
ridiculous.

She used to laugh at my jokes. Lately
it's all
speeches and deep thoughts and warnings.
She sighs and I
button myself back up.
"You aren't ready to read them," Mom says. "You are supposed
to be ready
at sixteen. We are always
ready. It's
your time,
but you're just so . . ." She
shakes her head and makes this gesture with her hand
like I am a bird in flight.

I'm not sure what's so serious
about a bunch of notebooks but I don't need one more

thing

telling me who I am,
telling me to be more
serious
or just   more.
I have
casting directors
and mothers
and best friends with long legs
and boys named Tyler
with wet lips and dirty baseball hats
for that.

"Was she good at acting?" I ask. "Was she
a star like me?" I
flip my hair and purse my lips and look up all

dreamily at the roof of our
sedan. I just want my mother to
smile.
I don't even need her to
laugh; just
god
one smile.

Instead she
sighs.

"I mean, I know I'm not
some star.
I was just,
you know,
being—" I start because suddenly I want to be
smaller
or at least for Mom to know I think I am
small and nothing and nobody.

"I know how you are," Mom says, and she sounds
tired,
so I don't ask her to
tell me who I am

but I would sure like to know.

Mimi, 2022

The thing
is
I want *this* version of my mother
this one
here
in the notebook
this
Tiffany
who is
silly and sweet and sad and trying her best to be
something
except she isn't sure what
and
yeah. This Tiffany
is one I can understand and
is an entirely different Tiffany than the one sitting downstairs
on the couch,
staring at the TV.
All these Barbie versions of Mom,
again,
turning me all
around
and upside down.
All I know
really is that
Feminist Hero Tiffany
is on the couch, leaning toward the newscasters
and trying to get her hair
in a certain kind of nonsexual

twist. And that Feminist Hero Tiffany
is so so so so so   far

from this one
in the notebook, this
Trying Her Best Tiffany or
Dreaming Her Dreams Tiffany,
Silly Faces Tiffany,
Bird in Flight Tiffany,
and I wonder,
can you miss someone
you never knew?
Can you miss the version of the person
that existed before you were born,
that is not even a
shadow
right now?

It is
too much and
I get a zap
of when we were in quarantine
and I missed both the life I had been living
and the future one that felt impossible
and the ones I'd never lived but should have. I had so much time
for
missing
then

and now, too, I guess,
the page of Mom's notebook open in my lap,
my fingers refusing to turn the page,
not wanting to lose

the Tiffany on this exact day in 1999
who is trying so hard to be what everyone wants,
not wanting to know
how she became the one downstairs
who asks me to be
someone else,
who doesn't see how hard
I am trying
too.

So I don't turn the page.
I don't learn if she gets the cereal commercial.
I don't see when she meets
Walter Bruce and what does
or does not happen.
I leave it open.
Place it aside.
And return to Betty.

Betty, 1954

"Well.
Then.
That's that,"
Mother says
when I tell her Peter
won't
be marrying
me.

We pack up in one day and one
long night.

We talk about
nice families
who want babies. We talk about
staying with a friend of a friend of a
friend
first,
for a few months until my bed
opens up at the
nice home for
girls like me.
We talk about
the importance of some future
where I am white-veiled and good at
typing.
Some future I will be allowed to have
if I   very quietly
do this

and then forget
all about it.

That future sounds

fine.

Except for the small problem
of how I love this baby.

I fold up the things I wear now,
but Mother packs dresses five sizes too big,
things that look like nightgowns.
"For later," Mother says,
before getting a little
misty.

"You're lucky
we were able to get a bed for you
at this place," she says. "They said they can take you
when you are seven months along.
It will be sooner than you think.
Just stay
quiet and
work hard
before you get there."

She has not even told me the name
of the woman whose home I'll stay in
first.

"You are so lucky," she says
for the hundredth time.

"Lucky would be
if Peter married me
and we had a family together," I say,
and I touch my belly
right where I imagine
the baby's heart
is.

"Betty. Please," Mother says,
and in those two words are a lifetime of disappointment and
something else
too.
Disgust.

The suitcase is full
but it all feels
fake,
like a story happening to some other
girl.

I guess
though
I am   some other girl
now.

So.

                        (On our way out of town we pass
                        kids walking to school

in shiny shoes and ironed skirts
and I think
I am supposed to be

there

with them
and Mother says,
"You're supposed to be there with
them."
But when she says it, it means
something

different than when I thought it.)

We cross the border,
leaving behind our state,
and the border is just an idea,
a line drawn on the road

but also
also
I feel us passing through it
like it is a cement wall
like it is the difference between then and   now
like it is the end of everything.

Betty, 1954

For three months I stay
inside
and I do everything
Mrs. Worther
tells me to do.

Laundry and cleaning windows and
giving bottles to her baby
who is
chubby and sweet and laughs when I
sing.

"You're good with her," she says.
But she looks like it
hurts
to say it.

I am
though
good with her. I know how to hold her
so that she gets sleepy
and what to do when she
cries. I don't even mind the sounds she makes that wake me up
or how everything is
messy
when she's around.

Sometimes
that baby

touches my belly and
smiles
and she is the only one who doesn't
shift and slide
away from the round reality of me.

When it is time for me to leave she
shrieks, missing me
before I've gone. The sound
sticks
and I feel the future   righthereontopofme.
It is hard to breathe.
Mother arrives to take me away
and Mrs. Worther shakes her head.
"A shame," she says to
all of me.

Betty, 1954

It is called the Bright-Weld Home,
but really everyone just calls it
the Home.
Tucked into a corner of New York City,
which is the perfect place to hide

                                        what you have done.

It is quiet
here
in the
loudness,

so many sounds
mixed together turn to nothing
eventually.

In New York the river isn't blue or green
but gray and brown,
the color of skyscrapers
and the bottom of the ocean,
and I'm a little bit   grateful
for the ugliness.

The city smells like things you throw away.

        (I know about being thrown away.
        I know about being at the bottom of the ocean.

I know about being less beautiful
than other rivers and other people in other
places.)

Mother helps me fold clothes
and put them in drawers.
She sighs at everything:
the wall
the dresser
the carpet

me.

"You can go," I say, when what I really mean is
please stay.
I suppose I think that she will hear the
wanting
beneath.
She is my mother,
after all.
"Well, good," she says. "I'm glad you're settled in."

The walls are all white.
It smells a little like
mothballs and
someone else's shampoo.

This is not the kind of place you can
settle in
to.

I wait for the hug
and the kiss on my cheek

or my hair, like she used to do when I was
small
and hadn't yet turned

bad.

Instead
Mother nods again.
Sighs again.
And
leaves
me
here.

In the Home we are our first names only;
we are our due dates
and the chores we have to do that day
and we are also the things we want to be
After,
the lives we will live
Later,
if we can somehow get through
now.

In the Home we are
every mistake we have ever made
and the many people we have disappointed,
and we are
the promise of forgetting
all of it.

In the Home
we are
tucked into cots that barely fit our

growing bodies,
and we are
fed so many kinds of cream and butter,
and we are told about kind families who want babies
and the one single path forward
which is to sign a paper
and walk away
so our babies can have good lives.

In the Home
we are
together and alone in the same

breath.

Betty, 1954

There is only one book
in the Home:

Peter Pan and Wendy

I've never read it.
No one ever read it to me.
I do not have
That Kind of Mother.

But I read it now.
"That's for children," the Woman in Charge says.
She is thin-haired and
thin-smiled
and thin.
She is not kind or unkind.
She is probably also not
That Kind of Mother.

"I'm a child," I say,
because I'm sixteen
and I deserve gentle and sweet stories
about magic
and how it can fix everything.

Even now, don't I deserve
a place called Never Never Land?

"No," the Woman in Charge says.

"Look at you," she says. "You are not
a child
anymore."
Maybe she means because of the baby.
Or maybe she is talking about
the way my body has always grown,
which is
a little wild
and a little full
and a little
too
obvious.

All the things Peter loved—

no

not loved.
Wanted
for a time
before remembering to want,
something

better
simpler
nicer.

In the book, Wendy's body doesn't curve
and she doesn't make mistakes
or let people make mistakes

upon her.

"If it's a girl, I'll name her Wendy," I say
to a girl named Nell
who is due the week before me
and who sometimes puts her hand on my belly,
waiting for the kicks.
I haven't had a friend touch me
like that
ever.
But things are different in the Home
than they are out
there.
In here it takes two hours
to become best friends.

Nell is now my best friend.
Helen is so long gone,
so far away,
I barely remember the shape of her mouth
or what her
mean words
sounded like.

"They won't let you decide," Nell says, though.
"You won't name the baby."

"But—" I say,
because that can't be right.
These are our babies.
I know because they are right here
beneath our ugly nightgowns,
kicking our
ribs.

"Trust me," Nell says.
And she
shudders.

There might be things I don't know
about my new best friend.
There might even be things
I don't know about
myself.

Betty, 1954

There is a doctor with a gray beard

                                in between
        my   legs.

"Babies having babies," he says.
His voice sounds
like the cigarette he just smoked
moments before taking my
blood pressure.

The smell makes me sick.
Everything makes me sick.

"They'll find the baby a good home," he says.
"A good family. The family it deserves."

It is not the first time
I've heard about
good families.

                        (I used to be from one.)
                        (I used to think I would have one.)
                        (But now I am bad.)
                        (Still. If I can't have a good family,
                        maybe I can still have a family
                        that is
                        mine.)

"Someone said that a girl a few months ago
kept her baby—" I start saying
the words I've been thinking,
playing with late at night,
the way I used to play with
Peter's last name and how it could hinge onto mine.

It's a different dream
now.

"Not hers," the social worker reminds me
as always.

"But. The woman I stayed with before. I took care of her baby
and she said I was—"
I know I am saying things that I am not
supposed to say
but they just keep
clamoring around,
so insistent,
that maybe these people are wrong and I could be
this baby's mother even though they keep telling me
I am
not.

"Why would you think of making such a selfish
choice?" the gray-bearded doctor says,
reaching   for another   cigarette.

"I'm her mother," I say.
The word feels wobbly in my   mouth
but also
true

ish.

"No," the doctor says.
"Mothers are not
little girls
who can't keep their legs   closed,
are they?"

It is
I'm pretty sure
a rhetorical question.

Except

also

I'm not entirely sure

what a

Mother

is.

                    (And if I'm not sure, couldn't it be
                    me?)

Betty, 1954

My mother and I are the same height—
tiny—
tinier than you are imagining—
and my mother
covers her body in all the same ways I do—
with sweaters
and wide skirts,
with apologies
about the size of her
breasts
and how they are absolutely wrong
for the size of
the rest of her,

apologies that aren't   said   aloud
but are there anyway,

the way the baby is here   but not;
     the way a room can smell like   cigarettes,   even if no
one is
smoking.

"Can't I talk to Peter again?" I have to ask
when my mother visits,
a *special visit*
that is just her and me and the social worker
talking and talking and
talking
about why I am so selfish and stubborn, why I am not
fitting in
following rules

doing what is best.

She looks
mad
to have been called in.
Mad
that I can't just
keep my mouth shut and do what they say.
Mad that the social worker is saying my attitude
is
dangerous
for the other girls.

"Betty," Mother says.
"Peter is getting married. Maybe if he was—but he's not. He
is
moving on and you
can move on
too. This is best for
everyone. You know this. We
talked about it."

We didn't
really
though
talk about it
or
anything.

"But—" I say,
the tears coming
because they know everything has already been
decided.

"There is nothing to
discuss," my mother says.
She was
once
a silent film star.

Or rather,
not a star exactly—

she was once in a silent film or two,
her face so precise
and lovely,
her eyes so able to
light up on command,
but

they are dull
now
because of
me.

"I want to be her family," I say
pointlessly
absurdly
because no one is
listening.

The silence is

l
o
n
g

and then it is gone and I am left wishing for it to return.

"I want a lot of things," my mother says.
"I want a new house
and a new
car
and I want to be taller
and I want a diamond necklace
and to have been a big star married to
Marlon Brando.
I want a lot of things."

It's
sad
but
perhaps not as sad
as right now. But I do not
mention that to her.
I do not point out
that those are impossible things
that she cannot control
and choices made
long ago,
but that my baby is

here now

and could be

mine.

(Before she leaves, my mother
leans in close.

"You have a whole life ahead of you," she says.
"This will all be a dream; this will be
forgotten;
this is what's best for everyone."
"Trust me," she says after a breath so big
it startles me.   (Everything about my mother
                            startles me today.)
"You can begin
again.")

Betty, 1954

Nell's baby comes
right before Christmas.

                    (From
              my room, I can see
          the Rockefeller tree lit up
      for someone less disappointing than
    me; for children who believe in Christmas;
      for good little boys and girls nestled into homes,
    waiting for Santa with cookies and milk and that certain
jumpy, delighted feeling of waiting for a perfect day. That
                        tree and its
                        lights
                        are not for
                        me.)

A Very Nice Family
is ready for Nell's baby
except Nell won't sign the paper.

Instead she
is put in a room on another floor
away from the rest of us
but late at night I visit her and she
curls around
my stomach,
crying in time
with my baby's kicks.

"I can't sign the paper," Nell moans,

and we both
hold on   tight
to the swell of my stomach
as the sheets
soak
with her blood
and milk
and sweat
and tears

and all the dreams we are
learning to

let

go.

Betty, 1954

It's Christmas,   I suppose.
But there are no presents.

There is a ham.
And a tree that they tell us to
decorate,
as if we are children who need an
activity.
They can't seem to make up their minds
about if we are children or
adults,
and I suppose I can't quite decide
which I am
either.
Both.
Or perhaps, really,
neither.

Nell can't decorate the tree,
isn't allowed anywhere near us,
but I find a secret moment in between moments
and bring her a cut of ham and a roll that would taste better
warm.

But Nell shakes her head at the very idea of
eating
surviving
celebrating
being.

"What do I do?" she says.
There is
the way I want to marry Peter and keep our baby and also
the thing the social workers say about how our babies deserve
better
and there are all the other girls who do what they are told
and they never come back here but we are told they are

happy.
There is how small this room is and how old it
smells
and how they keep telling us about
options
but then only offering
one.
There are the families who are waiting for these babies
and they are probably
nice families
and there are the people telling us we are not nice
and there are the boys who won't marry us
and there is the way none of this makes sense, like this whole
situation
is a box full of puzzle pieces
from all different puzzles,
impossible to
fit together.

"We're doing what we have to do," I say.
"No. We're doing what they say."
"Isn't that the same thing?" I ask.

My fingers are too swollen for rings;
my waist too wide for all my old
clothes.
I am a different version of myself,
but even this new person   here
doesn't know what to   believe
or who, exactly, to   be.

Nell shakes her head at all the things I don't understand
yet
but
will
soon.

The baby kicks me.
A baby I did not ask for
from a moment
I didn't exactly ask for
now being born in a place
I didn't ask to be
and even this body   this one, here
isn't one I ever wanted.
It's not one I ever would have chosen for myself,
but it seems to invite
a whole world,
a whole life,
that wasn't planned or decided upon or requested but just
is.

"They keep telling me I want this," Nell says. Her voice
the texture of
wood that hasn't been sanded—rough and
filled with splinters.

I think of Peter
and Mother
and Helen, too,
and
I wonder
when people will stop telling us what we want
for long enough to
listen
to us actually telling them.

Outside, the Rockefeller tree is still there. It is
bright and tall and maybe if I do what they say,
if I really, truly listen to everything and do it all
correctly,
maybe
then
that tree will be
for me
too.

I still like
trees and presents and even
cookies and milk and maybe I don't believe in
Santa
exactly
but I wouldn't mind seeing his
ruddy, full face
and telling him what I want

as soon as I figure that
out.

Mimi, 2022

The attic was dark but now it's
nearly light,
night turning to not-night,
while I'm lost in Betty's words.

There is so much about her that is
now and
present
but so much
too
that feels sort of long-ago and
wrong. Like the way she is in that home
and the way no one is acting like that baby
is connected to her.

I hope there aren't homes like that
anymore,
mothers like that, without choices.

At school,
Sophie talks about her birth mom
casually,
this person who is
family
that she sees once a year
and calls on birthdays and holidays, if she feels up to it.
She doesn't always feel up to it,
she says, with a shrug like there's more to say, but not enough
time for it right now.

"My birth mom lives in Arizona," she said
once
when we were talking about the desert. "She loves it there,
wears a lot of turquoise. It's
cool. We sort of walk the same way. I don't know, it's just
my family, you know?"

It does not seem like the girls at Bright-Weld
will get to tell their babies
about deserts or turquoise
or how this all happened
or how love and families aren't always
neat equations.

When I was reading, it felt like
I knew what I needed to do;
it felt like
Betty was telling me something

important

about who to be in the world
and how to live in this body
and how to love or not
and why we aren't ever quite
in charge of the things happening to us
and what that means for me
and Mom,
but that gray early-morning light
makes it all just
flat and sad

and   far away.

Betty is my great-grandmother, which feels   far away, too,
but maybe
isn't.

I think of the photographs on the mantel,
the generations of
us all lined up,
and how we are all variations on one another—
a smaller nose   here,
a poutier mouth   here,
hair that waves more than curls
or curls more than waves
but never stays flat and tamed;
all of us at least a little bit
wild.

I am waiting for something to be figured out,
except
maybe
no one
actually
figures any of it
out.

My grandmother,
Betty's daughter,
is named Wendy,
just like Betty said she wanted
when she was at that home,
which means Betty figured something out   I hope,
which was how to decide something

and to say it out loud
and to find a way to be a different person
than the one she was expected to be.

There are
so
many
more
notebooks,

but it's Christmas
and I want to somehow
make it feel
the way it used to.

I am not getting the answers I wanted
exactly
from these ghosts,
but I do feel
undeniably

haunted.

Mimi, 2022

Here I am,
like a kid
up before everyone else
on Christmas morning.

I don't know why.
Mom's not talking to me
and I don't want Eric to talk to me
and outside there is one
sole
photographer
smoking a cigarette and I'd like to tell him
that we deserve a break
one day
just a small break from people like him.

I take a photograph of
our tree,
which isn't decorated but is at least
here
and I don't know how—if it was Mom or Eric or
Santa or someone else who made sure we had one.

I can't stop thinking about Betty
looking out at Rockefeller Center,
bringing ham
to her best friend,
and waiting for something
to happen that would change everything.

God, I hope it
happened.
I hope she held on to that
baby,
to the things she wanted even though no one else thought she
should,
to the person she believed she could be and not the one
they were telling her
she was.

Maybe
whatever happened,
it even changed   me,
the past so far away and also so
close.

Ghosts
everywhere.

I take the photo of the tree and write a caption:

Christmas trees always remind me of
being a little kid. And don't we all need that
sometimes?

I think it's innocuous
enough,
except
right away someone posts
the photo of me
from when I was thirteen
at the party.
A little kid like this? they ask
from some anonymous account

with a profile picture of a cartoon carrying a gun,
and I try not to look at it,
like I have always tried not to look
at it,
my dress

u   n   b   u   t   t   on   ed

                   so my bra is
                   exposed

and my tongue
out
as if I like it
that way,
as if I am always doing this kind of
thing.

                   My heart just
                   crashes
                   at the sight of it
                   online for everyone to see
                   again,
                   unerasable, the worst part of me just always
                   available for everyone to see and judge and,
                   god, why won't that guy
                   with his stupid cigarette
                              just leave us alone?

"Why in the world would an innocent young girl
have a bra like
that?" Mom said
when she saw the photo:

the red lace bra, my tongue. "You obviously wanted
some boy
to see it."

There are so many things I can't ever remember:
like Mom's
middle name
and how many ounces are in a pound
and who wrote that book
about Christmas ghosts.
But I remember
those words.

I delete my whole post.
What's the point of pretending I'm living in some
winter wonderland
when everyone knows
who I am and what life I am allowed to live?
I guess
I have a destiny that was already written
before I got here,
written in dozens of
notebooks, then piled into boxes,
a curse hidden away in plain sight
and
god
I just want to post something sweet and easy about
holidays and trees
so that I can live
for an instant
in that world instead of this one
where I have to be
a photo on the mantel
of a girl whose future was written by

all the other
girls on the mantel.

Upstairs,
the diaries strain with stories about
who we are
or maybe who we could be or
who we should try not to be. And being in my own home is
starting to feel
a lot like it felt to be surrounded by photographers yelling at me
to
say something,
be something,
look some
way.

It is hard to breathe
here, just like it was
there.

Soon the sun begins to burn brighter and Mom and Eric
emerge,
a little bleary and blue.
"I said," Mom says, "I didn't want to see
her."
She is speaking to Eric
and I am the her
and it hurts in the sudden way of a toe
stub
or a
funny bone:
sharp and certain,
even though it feels silly to
cry from it.

I look out the window to see if the guy
with the cigarette and the camera
can see us or hear us or judge us
but he just sits and stares
at the front door,
waiting for us to come out.

"It's Christmas," I say, whispering just in case he can
hear. "I thought—"
"Who cares about Christmas?" Mom asks. "I mean, honestly,
who
cares? You're not
a kid
anymore,
Mimi."

It is impossible not to hear the *whoosh-whir* of echoes:
Betty being told the same
thing,
that she is not a kid,
and it was
wrong
when I read it and it is
wrong
now.

"I am a kid," I say, maybe for Betty and maybe for me
and maybe even for once-upon-a-time Tiffany and her
silly faces that her mother
hated.

Mom rolls her eyes and goes
back upstairs.
Eric follows

and I say it again
louder
to make sure they hear:
 "I'm a *kid*." And for a moment that is too short
and too wintery, even for winter,
I feel a trace of
okayness
about what I said to those reporters
and what I said online,
for not knowing how to be
exactly
in this impossible moment
when I am
really
just a kid.

I feel like Betty's shadow—
caught up in decisions I didn't make
and decisions made for me
and trying to figure out what to
do.

It's Christmas morning
sort of

and we could sit under the tree
and open presents

but that's not what happens.

Mom doesn't come down again,
waiting
I guess
for me to disappear

somewhere.
Eric wanders into the kitchen
at some point
to get
provisions:
toast and coffee and
a stocking he filled for her but not
of course
for me.

He vanishes back upstairs before I can ask him
what it is I'm supposed to do, anyway.
So I turn on the television to find out what is happening with
my mother.

Two women argue about
whether it matters that Tiffany Dovewick's own daughter
doesn't believe her,
even though I never said that,
and I wonder why every station isn't that
crackling TV fire instead:
pretending to be warm and bright,
forgetting that what makes a fire
beautiful
is the way that
the living room smells like the outdoors,
the way it warms your toes,
asking you to get close, then reminding you when you are
too close,
learning over the course of a
firelit day
to take your time and
slide closer, further, closer, further
for hours

the promise of something perfect
so near
so bright
so orange and red and raging.

Impossible to resist
but
never quite
becoming.

Mimi, 2022

Merry Christmas, I text Clinton,
and he says the same back,
noting there was no
exclamation point on mine.

It's not very Christmas-y here, I say. But I do not mention
Mom's face,
the comment online,
or Betty's notebooks and how I can't stop
thinking about her.
*It's Christmas-y
here*, he says. *Mom made
cookies
for breakfast and there's that perfect
pine tree smell.*

Trying to make me jealous? I ask.
Trying to make you curious, he says. *Come on over,
the more the
merrier. My mom goes kinda
overboard for holidays
ever since my dad died,
like maybe if she can fill the house with enough
lights and songs and presents and sugar,
she won't remember that he's
not here.*

That sounds really sad, I say. Outside
the photographer is still

smoking
waiting
watching
and that is
sad
too.
I am sad. And then I get
sadder
at the idea of being sad on Christmas
and I curl my knees to my chest
to keep all that
sadness
away.
It's hopeful. I guess, Clinton says. His knees are probably not
all curled in. He's probably just
sitting,
being
fine.
Hopeful in the sad way.
Or just sad but tinged with delusion.
I don't know.
I can't really read
my mom.
It sounds from the way he says it
like it's fine
to not know her.
Like he doesn't ever have to really try to figure her out,
and maybe I felt that way
once. Maybe before
the notebooks
and the lawyers,
or even further,
before the photo of me
and the quarantine with Eric

and the messy knot of us,
before I learned that she was a person named Tiffany
who was once sixteen,
who once threw parties and wondered if her body was
okay or
too much. Maybe
back then,
before I knew any of that,
I didn't care either, about the difference between her delusion
and her hope. Maybe I can
go back there
to that not-caring place.

I strain to hear her upstairs. She is
speaking,
saying something to Eric or a reporter or,
I don't know,
herself,
but definitely not
to me.

My head
pounds.

Can I come over? I ask. *Like, really? Can I?*
I have images,
automatic, reflexive ones,
about taking photos there:
me in a house thumping with holiday spirit,
me in a sparkly Santa hat drinking
eggnog,
singing Christmas carols in front of some piano.

I wonder,
though,
without the story I am telling everyone
about who I am,
who it is
I would actually be.

And like that,
I leave my phone
behind.

Mimi, 2022

Maybe he
didn't really think I'd come,
but I do,
in a red sweater and a red Santa hat
and these shiny
green
leggings
that are from some Halloween costume or late-night
shopping moment
that Mom has from time to time.

                    (I was going to wear
                    what I'd been wearing:
                    a gray hoodie over
                    this blue sweater that I stitched
                    old Girl Scouts badges onto. But
                    I felt a surge of
                    rage
                    at the idea that Mom and Eric
                    could just
                    decide
                    that there would be no Christmas.
                    Just like that.
                    So I
                    rage-dressed myself in
                    the holiday spirit.)

"Well. Look at you," Clinton says, smiling.
He can surely see

that I am puffy from
crying
and shaky from
everything,
because he pulls me into a bear hug I didn't know I needed.
"Christmas has arrived," I mutter, and maybe tears are going to
come
again,
but he spins me around so that I'm facing his home.
"Oh, it's been here. Trust me," he says.

And
I mean
shit.

Old-timey singers are crooning
"Have Yourself a Merry Little Christmas"
over the speakers,
but they are almost crowded out
by the singing Santa figurine—
his hips slide side to side in some sort of Santa dance.
Everywhere there are
wreaths and lights and nutcrackers and things that sparkle and
sing and shine and
smell like Christmas.

And in the middle of it all is a tree
so tall it scrapes the ceiling,
so crowded with ornaments it is begging to
droop.
And next to that tree is his mom,
who looks exactly like a mom
at Christmas,
with wavy brown hair pulled back by a sparkly reindeer-ears

headband
and a smile so big it makes me
tired.
She's got an apron
covered with flour and she's holding
I could not make this up
a tray of cookies.
They look
truly
superb.

"Mimi! I've heard so much about you," she says,
which is maybe not something she was supposed to say,
because Clinton
rolls his eyes and blushes and says, "Okay, all right, enough of
that."
I have to imagine
she has not watched the news
or doesn't know that I am Tiffany Dovewick's
terrible daughter,
because no one who knew that
would offer me cookies and a smile that
big.
"I'm so glad you could join us! We're
Christmas people,
you know?"
"I can see that," I say. "This is—I mean, wow."
"Clinton thinks it's a little overboard," his mom says. "I guess it
is,
but isn't this time of year an excuse to be a little
overboard?"
"Absolutely," I say
and I even mean it, because it's
a lot,

but also she looks truly happy
underneath the nervous energy. "I'm sorry," I say. "I know it's a
little
weird
to barge into a stranger's Christmas morning."
"It's lovely," she says, and I think
for her
maybe it is.
"Thank you. I needed—maybe you know who my mom is—
things are complicated."
"They almost always are," she says,
and that's when I know that yes,
she is a person who does over-the-top Christmases and looks like
the Platonic ideal of a mom
but is also
a real person
who says real things
about the world.

I keep my sweater on. My hat too.
It is true
the way my puffy eyes are true.
All of it
real
at once.

We eat cookies and listen to the music. We don't talk
much. Clinton and his mom open a few presents;
they are things like
socks
and lottery tickets
and candy bars.
"We used to go all over-the-top," his mom says,
like some apology she certainly doesn't have to give

Christmas-less me. "But what we really want
we can't
have,
so we just
get some little things that
help. Chocolate helps. Fuzzy socks too. You know, I bet I have
an extra pair.
I go a little
overboard
when I'm shopping."
"Oh, that's okay, I—" I start, but she's already
bounding up the stairs to find socks for me, and Clinton puts
his hand
on my thigh.
"Let her give you socks," he says. There are maybe
a thousand words

under

those words. They have to do with
I think
how much he and his mom
miss his dad
and also
maybe
what it means to have me here
and how nice this morning has been and
you know
I guess
also

how much someone like me might need
a pair of nice socks
right now.

And,
god,
I want them, actually. My own pair of fuzzy socks. And I get a
little
worried
that she won't find extras
after all.

But she's
beaming
when she gets back. She has found
two pairs of
fuzzy
lavender
socks
with tags still on.
They are

it sounds silly but

they are beautiful.

"Wow," I say. "I don't—I mean, thank you. These are—
I love them." My voice
hitches
and I start to

cry
because I have needed
so
so
so
so
much

and I can't get
most of it. But I get to have
these socks. And it's
something.

"My mother loved nice socks too," Clinton's mom says and
Clinton
nods,
remembering his grandmother fondly, I guess.
And I wonder what it would have been like
to be from a line of women who
loved socks,
who made sure you had the nicest, softest pairs. I wonder
how much we pass on,
knowing it is a lot,
wishing I had come from

this.

There is no mention
in the notebooks
of socks.
It's funny
the things that make your heart

break
and mend
and want to do better.

Like fuzzy lavender socks on Christmas morning.

Mimi, 2022

When I get home it's just Eric on the couch
waiting up for me
maybe
or just
waiting.

It feels like walking into another world,
a place Christmas
forgot.

"Where's Mom?" I ask. "I have something for her."
"She's asleep," he says. "But I'm glad you're here.
We should
talk."

"Haven't we already?" I ask. "Can we talk tomorrow? It's still
Christmas."
"Look," he says. "You're sixteen. You're
basically an adult.
So you need to know that this thing is getting
out of control. All day long it's reporters and lawyers
and, look,
look,
even the news,
see? Every few minutes they mention
her name."

I look.
And yes. There it is. The photo of my mom
and a worn-out reporter saying
worn-out things about her.

"Yeah," I say. "It's
a lot."
The socks in my bag suddenly feel
silly
and small.

"And those notebooks," Eric says.
I forget all about socks and
everything else.
"Notebooks?" I say,
I take my Santa hat off. Eric cannot know
about the notebooks.
"They're a real
issue. They're just up there
waiting for someone to
find out about them. If people—
cops, lawyers—knew they existed?
Well.
I figured I'd take a look while your mom was
resting. And Mimi.
Those notebooks. If I'd read them before—
I would have never let her say anything, accuse anyone.
She's been trying to tell us all that she's some
victim,
but if you read those notebooks. Well. You'll see. Your mom
wants to be some
public figure,
but there's
shit in those notebooks." He's shaking his head and wringing his
hands.
This
this
is how Mom's boyfriend
spent his Christmas. In our attic. Reading our notebooks.

And deciding
who we are.

The notebooks, I am sure, are just for the moms and daughters
lined up on the mantel.
Our matching smiles and shapes and little sideways head-tilts
that say
maybe
I'm not so sure
about what's being told to me
and asked of me
maybe it is in writing things down
that we start to see how
strange it all is.

"You've read her notebooks?" My nails find the insides of my
palms
and they
dig in,
trying to tell my body this isn't happening even though it
is.
I think about the way it felt to see my body
in that photo from the party,
all
exposed and wrong. This feels
a little like that. Like I want to scramble to
cover up
something that has already been
seen.
"Did my mom tell you to go up there? To read them? She
wouldn't—"
Eric
waves his hand around like the question doesn't matter.

"Desperate times," he says.
"She mentioned them
from time to time. I saw them when I was moving in and trying
to find a place for
my air hockey table
and your mom said she just simply could not let go of
those stupid notebooks." He
shakes his head. Like the idea of hanging on to our past is
ludicrous. "So, with things getting more
intense
here, and no one else coming out of the woodwork,
I knew what I had to do. And she needs to stop with all this
honestly
at this point. It's better for everyone. You know?"

And sure
yes
I do sort of want Mom to
stop telling her story,
stop putting us in the spotlight,
stop all of it.
I want her to go to Northside with me and eat pumpkin bread
and people-watch from the big picture window,
or ask me about why I don't seem to have friends
anymore
and if I'm okay with that,
and what sort of dress I'm thinking of making next
and whether I imagine it on some
runway in Paris or at a little boutique shop in a small town like
ours.
I want us to
shrink
way down
to the size of me and her

in a boxy house
wearing matching fuzzy socks,
drinking tea,
thinking about taking a walk in the rain,
maybe,
if we don't just stay
right
here.

Maybe it's
fucked-up
to want my mom instead of some
national hero
living in the house with me. Maybe it's
bad
to want something for me that takes something
from her,
from everyone,
I don't know.

I

don't know.

I just know how badly I
want it. How it is painful to even think about
pumpkin bread and long talks and listening to the rain.
How badly I want it
hurts. And how easy it is for other people to have it
hurts.

Once upon a time, it was easy for us too. There were blanket

forts and
movie marathons
and this old record player that she taught me to
love
and her spiky, sprawling voice
singing along with Joni Mitchell
and Fleetwood Mac
and all these
people who were from before her time
even
but who meant something to her
because of the way their voices catch on their words,
the way the truth can be hard to
get
out but when it finally arrives it is
beautiful.

I don't know what changed
exactly—
me, mostly. My body and the way people looked at it and also
the photos and the party and just being
not a kid anymore. And it
reminded her maybe
of the things she had tried to forget,
about the things that happen
when you are not exactly a kid
anymore, even if you still
sort of
want to be.

The thought is a hallway
that I don't quite want to go down,

a door I didn't mean to open,
because,
in part,
hating her is
easier
than whatever this is.

Mimi, 2022

It's time to try

again.

Because it's Christmas
and a stranger gave me soft socks
and I am tired of hating my mother
when something else
is right here.

In this box.

This box that Eric
has already opened.

Tiffany, 1999
Typecasting

I thought maybe I'd be good in
comedies or as a really fun
zany best friend
or even like
on some kid's show where I could sing and dance and be
sort of embarrassing and silly. But.
I am hired to be
the girl who was killed
by the man in the ski mask
on her sixteenth birthday
because of the low cut of her top
and the way she smoked cigarettes
and flapped her eyelashes

I am hired to be
the girl who kills a young family
because of her drunk driving—
reckless and raccoon-eyed—
because
bad girls wear
dark eyeliner.

I am hired to be
the babysitter that the father fantasizes about

and

the cheerleader everyone hates

and also

the kind of pretty, kind of vapid girl who shows up
in photos in a math textbook
the one who probably doesn't know any of the answers

and also

the girl who makes you do
Bad Things
like steal and lie
and kiss someone else's boyfriend.

I start to wonder:
If you wear dark eyeliner
and have a body that spills up and over
and out,

is that the same as being
the girl who was killed and the girl who kills and the babysitter
who tempts and the girl who makes you
do

Bad Things?

Yes, they say on the phone, asking me to be
the girl who
is found at the party
with her shirt unbuttoned,
red bra
exposed;
her hair covered

in puke.

Yes,
that is who you are.

Mimi, 2022

It is hard to shake the words

red bra.

My skin feels
cold and dry and also hot and damp and my brain won't think
anything but those two words
red bra
red bra
red bra

I think it so many times in a row that it starts to make me
nauseous or dizzy or
both. I shut the notebook and open it again. And shut it again.
And

throw it across the room.

And go to where it has landed
to open it
again.

Can you be scared of something that has
already happened,
of a history that has already been
lived?

I am
scared
to follow this thread from her to   me,

    from then to   now.

Tiffany, 1999

They do not hire me to be
the girl who has a sweet first kiss
on her sixteenth birthday to the stylings of
Dave Matthews Band
or the girl who laughs a little too loudly
at the teacher's jokes, and then makes
some of her own.

They do not hire me to be
a girl who smiles
at babies in line at the
grocery store,
making
funny fish faces, wiggling fingers, wishing I could
pinch their chubby
toes,
or the girl who
can sing
the entire soundtrack of *Rent*
without missing
a
beat,

so maybe
I am not
that girl

after all

Tiffany, 1999

On set,
when I am playing
a part with no lines,
the Girl Who No One Likes Because She Steals Boyfriends,
the director
points at me;
asks his
camera guy
who
I
am.

"Some girl," the camera guys says,
shrugging,
as if I can't hear him.

"A very pretty
girl," the director says. And it feels

good?

It's good to be
a pretty actress,

so it must be good
that he called me one.

"Come here, Some Pretty Girl," he says,
two of his fingers insisting.
I go to him and can't decide if I should introduce myself or
just stay silent,
so I

start a sentence

I never

                         finish.

                                    "Oh, I'm, hi, do you . . ."

      He   grins.

"You don't have to be nervous," he says.
"Oh, okay," I say. "Thanks. I'll just
stop." I laugh at my own little joke.
"What's your name?" He does not laugh. Pretty girls aren't really
supposed to be
silly; I have been told more than once.
"Tiffany."
"Of course it is." He grins again. I don't know what any of it
means
and my heart pounds

and I think I'm supposed to want
this
attention,
so I tell my body to
relax and enjoy.
"I'm Walter," he says. "Which I assume you know."
"Walter Bruce," I say, like it's some
pop quiz
where the right answer is his full name in my mouth.
"I like you," he says, even though he didn't like my joke and
knows
nothing else about me.
"Oh. I. Great. I like you too?" My voice is
small
and I am blushing and I don't think this is how
actresses
are supposed to be, so I
try again.
"Sorry," I say. "I'm nervous. But I'm, you know, honored you
even noticed me."
This
was
right.
He
grins.
"I sure did," he says. "You have an interesting
look. The blonde curls. You look a little
fairylike. All small
but also
sexy; it's an interesting
combination. That's good in this
business, Tiffany.
To be the right kind of interesting.
And I was thinking

maybe
you need some lines.
You think you could do that? Do some acting with
words
and not just with

your body?"

It is,
it must be,
a really good thing,
right?
It is me
an actress
getting to act
and it is good and I tell my heart to
like it
and to not think about
the way he   dwells
     on the word   *body.*

"I would love that," I say,
which is true,
and when I get the lines they are
fun and snarky and light and lively
and I know how to say them
and I say them just that way.

This is it, I think. *I am acting. In a movie.*

Walter Bruce   grins again. He is a person who
grins instead of smiles.
And it feels
not exactly the way I thought it would
to have the cameras trained on me,
to say the words written just for me,
to have them all
looking at me.
Not exactly the way I thought it would,
but then,
nothing ever feels
quite the way you imagine:

kisses from Tyler or getting the lead in the school play or
wearing a prom dress or throwing a sixteenth birthday party
or drinking beer with Rachel or dancing with someone who
touches your ass or wearing a thong or getting your period or
being right here and right now
being a girl
none of it
feels
the way we were promised it would.
And little by little
I guess
I have gotten used to that space
between what I thought it would be and what it

is

so by the time the day is over

and Walter Bruce is
maybe
looking a little too long
at my
chest,
it's like anything else,
really—

not what I thought it would be
but
I guess
what it is
what it has to be
what I need to accept.

So I do.

Mimi, 2022

This time
I don't throw the notebook, but I
put it down gently and move my hands away fast and
look somewhere else. Out the window. To the tops of trees that
I've never really looked at before. I
try to get lost in them. I try to live in them
for a second. Trees don't know the name
Walter Bruce.

I think I'd like to stay here forever, looking at trees and not
thinking about anything else.
That would be easier, wouldn't it? That would be
better? Than knowing things you thought you wanted to know
but actually now
really wish you didn't?

It's like.
When you're seven or eight and you want to know what it will
be like
to be
older,
to be
some girl with boyfriends and high-heeled shoes and
algebra tests
and red bras. And there's just no way

(but *fuck* I wish there
was)

to tell that seven- or eight-year-old girl

that maybe they don't
want to know.

My fingers itch to
tell someone something, to not be alone
with just the trees and these
notebooks, but I am
alone.

Trees are terrible companions and Mom is hiding and Eric is
awful and Clinton
would never understand what I am finally understanding, which
is that

bodies aren't lawless spaces
like Mom said.
They are
cages,

places we are trapped inside,
and the world just gets to
look and
decide
who we

are.

I guess that's the
lawless part.

I ready myself to go back downstairs
to face Eric or
go to sleep or
maybe crawl into bed with Mom like I used to when I was little
and having nightmares,
but before I put the notebooks away
a page flips
by itself,
opening up to some new
moment she recorded,
some new bit of history
I both want to know
and desperately
do not want to know.

Really what I want
is for history to be
different. Really that is why I keep
looking at the trees instead of reading. Really that is why I keep
putting my head in my hands,
closing my eyes,
imagining who I would be if I could be someone
else.

Tiffany, 1999
The Way It Feels to Not Really Know Your Own Mother

[*Romeo and Juliet*
The House on Mango Street
The Bell Jar
The Fountainhead
The Handmaid's Tale
I Know Why the Caged Bird Sings
Valley of the Dolls
A Little Princess
Their Eyes Were Watching God
Great Expectations]

a list of books
in Mom's office
that I steal away

to read
in our car at night
down the street
from the house on First and Flower
like a Volvo   can become
a hideaway
a home

Every few pages—

a clue,
sometimes a penciled heart,
a scribble of words
so ecstatic
they can't be   deciphered.

Most often:
                         YES!

underlined
twice,
three times,

louder on paper
than I have ever heard
Mom's   voice.

          sometimes, sometimes I find myself nodding at
          the very same things
          that my mother, long ago, underlined three times

          and it is maybe the closest we have ever/will ever

          be

There is school and
auditions and
Walter Bruce calling to ask if I'd like a small role in
something else,
and there's Rachel's incessant chatter about nothing
and Tyler sometimes acting like my boyfriend,
and there is this:

me. in the car, reading words my mother read,
wondering if she ever felt this way,
like something is   wrong
      even when everything is   right.

But there is also this:
I try to ask my mother, "When you were my age, did anyone
ever—"
and she
shakes her head. "When I was your age
I was nothing like you. I wasn't trying to be some actress. Things
were
serious, Tiffany." And she
sighs
so that I know how very serious and real she is and how very
not serious and not so real me and my problems are.

She is right.
I am not a serious girl. I have always been
silly and light and fluffy.
And the things that feel
weird and jagged inside me
are nothing at all. They are nothing at all. They are
imagined problems from a silly girl.

So I call Walter Bruce back.
"I'm so
amazed
that you thought of me," I say,
keeping my voice
breathy. Letting myself
giggle.
"You have no idea
how much I've thought of you," Walter Bruce says,
so I

giggle

again,
the way silly girls
always do.

Tiffany, 1999
The Way It Feels to Not Really Know Yourself

When Tyler kisses me again
it is
hard
behind the school
with wet lips
and not seen by anyone.

I sort of wish
there were an audience
so that the kissing could make sense,
could feel the way kissing is meant to feel:
purposeful,
urgent,
wanted.

Instead
it is only

wet,

uncomfortable like a bathing suit stuck too long
to my body
the way it used to be
after days at the lake
when Mom was
happy
and Dad was

here.

Tyler's kiss is
wet without water
wet without wishing
wet without wanting.

"Oh," I say into his mouth
"Oh."

Tiffany
The Way It Feels to Not Really Know Who They Want You to Be

"You need new
headshots," Walter Bruce says when I show up
at the audition. "These ones
they don't capture
you."

Walter Bruce's shirt is pressed and he plays with his
watch. He rubs his forehead. He looks busy and
tired.

"You need to show
sexy fairy energy," he says. "Sultry wood nymph.
That's
your type."

"Oh, okay," I say. "I didn't know."

The way he looks at me makes me feel
small,
but, I mean,
I am small,
so maybe that's okay. Besides,
next to him is a
woman, a casting director, in a light blue
sweater,
and she has blonde highlights and pink lipstick and she
nods at the things he's saying. She taps a pencil on the table and

half smiles at me.

I read the two lines the character I'm auditioning for has
and Walter Bruce shakes his head.
"Not quite right," he says,
but he doesn't tell me how to make it
better.
So I just
stand there
and wonder if I stick my hip to the left and my chest forward,
if I separate my lips like models do,
if I wear something
tighter or lower or shorter or flashier,
would that make me more
right? My eyes flit to the woman in the blue sweater,
but she's looking
past me.

"Maybe next time, Tiffany, okay?" he says.
"Right, yes, okay, next time," I say, but it isn't okay.
And I don't feel like there's going to be
a next time. This is the time.
I want him to look at me
again
the way he looked at me on set. I want him to see
whatever he saw
that day
and for him to know I am a
serious actress,
not the silly nothing-girl my mom thinks I am.
I can do this,
I can be this person,
I can be any kind of person.
That's, like, what being an actress

is.

"If there's anything I can
do
differently,
let me know? I'll do the
photos,
the sexy, um,
fairy ones, and,
you know,
I'd just really love the chance to
work with you again."

Walter Bruce
tilts his head.

"Good to know,
Tiffany. I look forward to seeing
those photos."

I tilt my head
back
and

smile.

Mimi, 2022

One thing I am learning
right now
in this attic
is that memories can be really

very

loud.

Mimi, 2022

I leave the attic.

There is so much more to read, but I

can't.

It is still   somehow   Christmas.

          It is still   somehow   the day I went to Clinton's home,

where nothing is like it is here,
where a whole other kind of life is being lived.

It feels
unfair. And for a moment I
let that unfairness swallow me up. Some people get *that* and I
am left with

this.

But.

Underneath one hundred pounds of
tinsel and holly and
pine,
there was the way Clinton's mother kept saying that
mint chocolate cookies were her late husband's favorite
and how no one actually ate

them.
There was the spot on the wall that Clinton looked at
when I asked about a hockey-playing Santa ornament,
and there is the way they didn't seem to want me to leave.

What if I actually hate Christmas? I text him.
That would be fine, he texts back.

I wait. Maybe what the notebooks are trying to tell me
is to trust no one
and especially not some guy.
But, I want to feel sure about something
and maybe that something could somehow be
him.

*I think
the thing my mom said happened
with the Walter Bruce guy really did
happen*, I text.

It's not a test
exactly
but I'm nervous that he's going to
fail. Downstairs is a man who is supposed to love my mother,
who read these words she wrote when she was sixteen
and he only saw the way she
giggled and wore red and tried to be what he wanted her to be.

Shit, Clinton replies. I have no idea if that was the right response
or not. So I don't know how he did
on the test that wasn't a test.

I tell him about notebooks in the attic anyway.

I don't know how much I want to know.
It goes
back and back
my mom and hers and hers and hers. It's just this
collection of
secrets
or
things I didn't know
like how when you are in history class
and your teacher is all
"this leads to this leads to this, and that's why the pandemic was as
bad as it was
and that's why Black Lives Matter is a necessary movement
and that's why this president won this time and that one the other
time
and that's why we went to the moon when we did
and joined the war when we did
and protested when we did." you know?

I have always liked
history
and how it's a little more like math
than anyone ever tells you.

What are you trying to learn? Clinton asks.
It's a good question
and I don't have
an answer. *Maybe you don't have to*
try so hard.
Maybe just come back over here
and kiss me on the couch
and stop trying to figure out
how everything in the world led to this right now.

I think
he thinks
he's being sweet.

I think
he thinks
I am that girl online
who buys cute clothes and wants a boyfriend;
that girl online
who posts song lyrics and inspirational messages and teaches
everyone how to
do complicated braids or wear just enough
eyeliner.
That's the girl
he liked.

He probably
even
liked the girl in the red bra
with her tongue sticking out.
That is probably
what he signed up for. That is
what they all sign up for:
sexy trashy fairy with a
red bra.

I don't know what you think this all
is
but my mother is
hiding in her bedroom
because of something that probably
definitely
happened
a long time ago

and the answers are
literally
right here. And I can't figure it out
because the person in these fucking notebooks
isn't the same as the person lying in her bedroom
and god you do not
get it
at all
or get me
at all
and this is why I don't
do the friend thing.

There is a long
pause.
Maybe I should have waited to press send, should have reread
and made it
nicer
but my fingers
flew
and I am tired of the way my life seems
unserious
to everyone

even him.

The pause   goes   on.
It doesn't end.
Clinton does not
text
back.

Mimi, 2022

It is not the first time I have
sent texts
that no one answers,
that hang in the air
too long.

I am not good at
people.

I am not good at
being a person people can love or even really
like.

Maybe
none of us are
none of us girls from the mantel
with our curlyish hair
and fairyish faces
and bodies that say
look look look look look
but also

don't.

These are my friends,
I guess,

these

ghosts.

Betty, 1954

Nell stays for three more days.
She just keeps
not signing
the paper.

Nell and I do not talk
again about
what is happening or how we feel about it
or whether we even wanted
any of it.
We do not talk about
the baby's tufts of hair
or
how cute she might be
or
what Nell would like to name her.

Instead
we sit in Nell's room
and talk about what we will wear
to the spring dance
in our hometowns:
what color dresses
and what kind of jewelry
and what style of shoes.

"You'll go with your guy?" Nell asks.
He has never come up before.

I take a breath before
answering.

"He's not mine," I say,
and it feels
so empty and sad.

"But maybe when you get back—"
Nell starts.
"No. He's with someone else."
"Someone else?"
"She's pretty. Sweet. She's good. A good girl."
Nell nods.
We both know about good girls
and how we are not
good
girls
now.

I look around Nell's room.
It is solid white
like mine,
like everyone's,
and cracked ceilings,
and the draft through the window
that looks out at nothing
except another building
with more sad girls inside,
probably.

There are sad girls
everywhere,
if you think about it.

"Maybe they'll break up," Nell says.
"Maybe," I say, and I accidentally let myself hope
for one minute
that Peter will come back
and talk
again
about lake houses and
coffee in the mornings
and what he thinks of my
eyes.
"He gave me this. Once," I say, holding up the heart charm
around my neck.
Maybe I shouldn't be wearing it,
but I am.
Nell leans in,
inspects it.
"He loves you," she says.
And
oh, wow
do I want it to be
true.
I want it to be true enough that he comes here
and tells me we can be
the good family
that this baby deserves.

There is a long pause.

It hurts.

My baby kicks
and that hurts too.
Somewhere
else
Nell's baby coos
or screams
or continues to nap on the chest of someone
who isn't here.

That, I am certain, hurts the most of all.

"I'm going to our dance with my guy," Nell says
when the pause is over,
or maybe
just when she needs it to be.
"He said he'll take me out to a fancy dinner first
he said I should wear pink
he said he's going to learn how to dance
he said there will be a corsage
he said it will be the most beautiful night of our lives."

There is another long pause.

It is the pause of a decision being made or
no
it is the pause of understanding
you are not being given a choice.
It is the pause between where Nell pretends she might raise her
baby
and where she realizes
no one was going to allow that

anyway.

My baby hiccups inside me,
a strange and otherworldly feeling
that no one told me about,
but then, I guess
no one told me about
any
of
this.

Nell waits in bed
for the bleeding to stop
for her legs to work
for her body to change
back
into what it used to be.
She waits in bed hoping to believe that
she can wear a pink dress
and a pink corsage
and a boy on her arm.
And that that will be
enough.

I want it for her.
I want it for me too, but that's
silly
because I am not going to have any of those
things.

Not now.
But also
I am suddenly so sure
not ever.

"Maybe I won't go to the dance at all," I say. "Maybe—"
I don't know how to finish the sentence because Nell is telling
me to get the social worker,
she is telling me she is ready to sign the paper,
she is choosing a path because it is the only path that anyone
will show us
and we are too young,
we are just girls,
we can't walk on a hidden path
without any light on it
that everyone is telling us
doesn't exist anyway.

When Nell leaves the Home she doesn't look back,
doesn't reach for my hand
or whisper sage advice in my ear.
She doesn't say goodbye at all,
as if all of this never happened.
As if
I
never happened.

It wouldn't be the worst thing in the world,
now that I think about it.

Mimi, 2022

We shouldn't
have ever
started this,

I text Clinton, even though he has said exactly

nothing.

I don't want to get all
tangled up
in a thing.

it's not worth it.

it never is.

Mimi, 2022

"See?" Eric says
when I come back downstairs.
It is at least two in the morning,
three, even.
I didn't think he'd be up.

"See what?" I ask.
"See what I mean
about your mom,
about all the stuff in there that no one needs to know?"
My spine stiffens having to think
again
of Eric reading
our words. The words that belong to
us and so deeply not to him.
"Which stuff?"
"She went after him.
The guy.
The Walter guy.
You're reading it, right? She
wanted to be famous and she used what she had, and
if they find that shit out,
she's gonna look real bad."
Eric shakes his head, sighs. He talks like he's talking about
some idea of a person who shows up on the news. He talks
like he's talking about
Tiffany Dovewick, Accuser,
and not
Tiff,

the woman who gives him foot rubs
and
makes him sandwiches to take to work
even though she never makes me
any sort of lunch.

His back is to me so he can't see the way my whole body
tenses
coils
wants to explode.

"That's what you—
you read her notebooks and that was your
conclusion?"
I wonder if he can hear it in my voice,
the barely-holding-back of it all.

He whistles some song

whistles!!!!!!

and I wonder what it would feel like to
rush at him
and just
s   h   o   v   e.

But I don't. I shove
instead
my
mouth open and the words
out.

"She was sixteen. She was sixteen and had no idea what was
happening. I mean. That's what she wrote. You must have—"

"Sixteen's not always
sixteen," he says, as if the laws
change
based on what someone does or how they
look
when they do it.
"And I'm sure you've read enough
to go upstairs
and tell her to stop all this. She can
withdraw her
statements, I'm sure,
go back to just being
herself,
just being there for us. For you and me. Stop making everything
so
complicated."

The thing is
she didn't make things complicated. Things just *are*

complicated.
I put a hand on my heart to slow it down, to slow down
all the thoughts pulsing through me.

The phone rings.
I answer and it's another reporter
calling in the middle of the night
like that is a thing
real reporters do. She's from some
other magazine

wanting another quote about my mother. "Am I speaking with the famous
Mimi?" she asks.
"I'm not famous," I say.
"You have quite the following online! Right in your mother's footsteps, hm?"
"I'm not an actress."
"You might as well be
twins.
I'd love to hear more about you and your mother's interests
in being in the public
eye."

I hang up.
And go upstairs.
and I sleep the tiny tail end of Christmas
away.

Mimi, 2022

"Not now, Mimi," my mother says
the next morning
when the door has only barely
squeaked   open.

The news is on
even in here,
promising more women coming out
against Walter Bruce,
but they don't come
don't share their names
don't have photos up on the screen.

"God, where *are* they?" Mom mutters
to herself.

"The phone is still—" I try,
"and Eric seems kind of—
I'm trying to understand
everything,
but you didn't give me much information
and now it's all this big mess,
but it's not completely
my fault,

I don't think,
that I didn't know
how exactly to do
this."

Mom rolls over so I can
finally
see her face. It's
puffy.

There is
then
a clip of Walter Bruce himself. He is
handsome
in a certain type of way that,
like,
grandfathers
might be handsome. He is the memory of
handsome.

"Mom? I read your
notebook. From
then. Or part of it. From the start of
stuff."

I don't have an
agenda,
saying it. I just have the knowledge of it bubbling up and
out
and the wanting to Eric to leave so that we don't live in a house
with someone who thinks
sixteen means something different
than what I am starting to think
sixteen might mean. I just have

the knowing it's impossible to sit with it alone
and the having no one else to go to
and the way that Tiffany feels like a friend even though Mom is
something else.

Mom turns off
the television.
The lack of sound draws attention to the way the room smells,
stale and wrong.
It feels colder,
too,
like the heat isn't quite reaching her bedroom. My toes
chill.
And my earlobes.
There's also
the neighbor's giant singing Santa outside
playing "Jingle Bell Rock" on repeat,
something Clinton's mother
would love.
Cars drive by on icy, sloshy streets,
and that noise, too, feels far away and
of another world.

Up here it is just me
and Mom.

"We haven't talked in
forever, maybe. But
it was Christmas and I was alone up there and you're in here and
Eric is,
come on,
a fucking asshole,
and I think I had this boyfriend,
maybe,

but I just couldn't
do it, like how Betty knew
that she wasn't going to get to go to that dance
with Peter,
even after everything,
and I just need someone to

see me. Can't you? See me,
I mean? And I can try to see you and we can
be the same,
right? Like what happened to me at that party
and what happened to you with
um
the guy? Isn't it—
aren't we the same? Can't you
see me? Isn't that why we have the notebooks
anyway? To see
each other
finally?"

But.

"Where's Eric?" Mom says, her voice
cracking and cratering.
"He's downstairs," I say. "And he thinks you should
call it off or something? Is that even
something you can do? He thinks,
I don't know,
I guess he thinks maybe it was sort of

your fault. Or something."
I
watch Mom's face for

rage, maybe, or
some sort of
fuck you energy
or
passion or
even
agreement. I don't know. I don't know.
I'm overwhelmed and looking for
something to grab on to.
And I want to grab on to
my mom.

I sit on her bed.
It's cozy. I haven't been in here
much
since Eric moved in. I slide next to her,
lining my body up
next to hers. We used to
read books in here,
watch Disney movies, singing along to the best parts. We used
to
have tea parties made of air
in here,

and she would tell me all the things
she wanted me to be.

Maybe,
I think,
she will tell me again
what it is I might become. Maybe she will tell me
how to feel and what to do and that everything will be

okay.

"You really loved
acting," I say, feeling dreamy and
daughter-y. "Were you good? I bet you were good. And you
were,
I don't know, you sounded like fun. We would have been
friends,
I think,
if you weren't
my mom." I close my eyes and try to find the pace of her breath.
It's safe here
in this place I used to know well and haven't been since I got
boobs, and my account, and a shitty
step boyfriend
or whatever you'd call
Eric. It's safe and we have
so much to talk about
finally.
"Eric said those notebooks were
dangerous,
the things in them,
like,

bad for your case? But he's
wrong, Mom,
he's totally—
he's wrong. I haven't read it all, but from what I saw—"

"Eric read them?" Mom says.
She sounds
confused, sitting up in the bed
like she is
lost in the cotton and
quilted
covers.

"I guess."

"And he said they're—they're bad for my case? They're
bad?"
Mom
bites
her
lip.

"I guess, but he's totally wrong because I read a little and—"

"Don't read any more," Mom says.
"But you told me to read—"
"I haven't read them in
ages
and you shouldn't either.
None of us should
Eric too
but none of us
that's
the past, and I was

god
I was so
wrong. And our family with its stupid
notebooks filled with
filled with
things we don't say for a reason.
We don't say these things
for a *reason*, Mimi."

"No, Mom, I'm telling you the entries I read,
you were totally
right. Walter Bruce was totally disgusting and it wasn't your— "

But Mom just
shakes her head, like somehow Eric knows more than
me
more than
her
about her own
past
about all of us,
really.

(When the photo of me
in the red bra
showed up
it was Eric who first called it
bad, and it was Mom who
agreed. She looked
the same then as now—
out of place,
unsure of
how she arrived.)

"Don't write
another word," she says. "Tell Eric
I need to see him. Tell him
I need to talk to him about
everything."
"Mom. Don't talk to Eric about it. He doesn't know—"
"Mimi, please. I can't. It's too hard."

I don't know if she means
this conversation or
accusing Walter Bruce or
standing up to Eric or just
being
being a Dovewick girl, being a person in a body in this house in
the world
who people notice and see and
judge.

"We can read them together. The notebooks. We can
figure it all out. I have other questions, too, about
Betty and
Wendy and,
I mean,
me. I have—"
I am talking
fast,
desperate, the way I've seen girls do
at school when they want someone to
like them
choose them
let them stay. It is how girls who are trying too hard
talk to the popular girls. It is

embarrassing.

Mom shakes her head.
"It's too hard," Mom says
again.

So I leave
slink
shrug
out the door
not wanted there or
anywhere.

But
the attic is
right
there. Telling me

there's

more.

"Mom wants to
see you," I tell Eric,
passing him in the kitchen. He has
mayo on his lips, he is
eyeing the reporters outside, he is
looking in the paper at a photo of
Mom and Walter Bruce, and he is
deciding
something.

I don't wait for him to
say yes or no or wipe the mayo
away. I don't need to hear anything more
from him.

I go upstairs
quietly
like it's a secret
except I'm

really

fucking

tired of secrets.

Betty, 1954

They do not
go to the hospital with me,
not the Woman in Charge,
not any of them.
They
put me in a cab
and tell me
to
be a good girl.

I don't know if I
am good or not
because when I arrive I tell them I am from
the Home
and they
rush me into a room
and quickly I

disappear.

When I come back
she has been born.

Betty, 1954

Just once
I see her
all scrunched up and screaming
in the nursery.

"Which one's mine?" I ask the social worker
with the pronounced chin
and New York accent
who walked me to the nursery.
She says
"None of them, sweetheart,"
and it is a kind-meanness
or a mean-kindness.
"That's the one you gave birth to," she goes on,
crueler and kinder still,
and points at the wailing willow of a baby,

so small and so
loud.

"I want her to be named Wendy."
"Her parents will name her," the nurse says. "You can name your
own daughter
Wendy
someday."

Somewhere in the middle of the sentence
an essential part of me
slips

away.
Surrenders.
Becomes someone else
entirely.

just
like
that

I want to know the color of the baby's eyes
and the shape of her hands,
but the social worker turns me away.

"Sign the paper," she says, putting a pen in my hand.
I try to
speak, to tell her
again
about Mrs. Worther's baby and how I am
good with babies
and I want to tell her that my baby
lying in that little bassinet
is so beautiful I almost can't breathe.
I want to tell her that
Peter said my eyes are like the ocean
and that means something. I want to tell her
that I miss having the baby inside me, and I'm scared to
walk away all
empty.

I feel
like I'm on one side
of a huge river
and I can see the other side—it's right there
and it's so lovely and green and sunny over there. But

no matter which way I go
no matter where I look
there's no bridge
no path
no way I can get
to that other side of the river
where there's all that sun.

I'm stuck
here
with a pen in my hand and a social worker
saying over and over and over
that I agreed to this
that this is what I wanted
that I know
what I have
to do.

"Sign the paper," she says
so many times I lose count.
 "Start over."
"You're young."
"This is for the best."

And I do.
And I will not.
And I am.
And yet it is not
for the best.

Betty, 1954

The drive home is either
long
or maybe
short.

And I am
fine
or maybe
not fine at all.

"I wanted to name her Wendy," I say to my mother
when it has been two hours
or four
or none and I cannot stop thinking
about that pen
and that paper
and how I somehow
somehow
somehow
let my hand
make the shapes
of my name.

"You'll name your own baby Wendy," Mother says,
just like the nurse did,
in the kind of voice
that walks a tightrope.

"But she was my own—"

My heart
unspools into something wild and
scared.
"No. Enough with that." It's my father this time.
He is finally here in the car.
He is finally a part of this except also
not.
It is the loudest his voice has ever been.

So I quiet
on the outside
but nothing inside me
will ever
ever
be
quiet
again.

Mimi, 2020

My grandmother is named
Wendy.

I met her once
and only that
once.

Mom said they were never
close
and that seemed like a nothing statement
at the time
but now
I wonder if any of us are
close. I thought for a moment
we could be
again
close in that bed and looking at shadows on the wall while we
said
what we were afraid of or who we
wanted to be.
Instead Mom's there with Eric and we're all just holding on to
these
things
about each other, these secrets in the notebooks,
the names of people we kissed and whether we
liked it,
and the kind of alcohol we got drunk on
that first time,
and who touched us when we wanted to be touched,

and who touched us when we
did not.

The other Wendy,
maybe,
is gone, the one who is named something else
entirely, who lived some other life.
She probably never kept
a notebook.
But maybe she had a family
and maybe they are
somewhere. I try to picture them now,
the day after Christmas,
playing with,
I don't know,
model airplanes or new video games or giant five-thousand-piece
puzzles.
In my head they look like Clinton's family,
or some happier version of Clinton's family,
where there's two parents and a bunch of kids and crumpled-up
wrapping paper everywhere
and probably
like
a dog.

I miss her, the way I have learned you can find a way to miss
someone you never knew. I miss her for Betty
and for Mom and me, too, for everyone who read about her and
hoped
she belonged to us
only to find out she is
on someone else's
mantel,
part of someone else's
story.

(But ours too, isn't she?)

I almost want
for a moment
to be in that other not-Wendy's family,
the one without all the secrets in the attic.
I am getting
h   e   a   v   y
with these secrets,
all of them written in perfect little
lines,
and we are
cursed,
aren't we,
with the things we are meant to hold but never
talk about,
the story of how we got here so big that it doesn't leave room
for card games at Christmas or twelve people around a table at
Thanksgiving
or
even me and Mom just
side by side
being okay in the same space at the same time.

All the secrets
pile up,
lay themselves out between us,
make it impossible to
see,
like we are
just like Betty,
squinting across some impossible
valley

or ocean or
attic filled with notebooks of things we refuse to say
out loud.

Those stupid girls
on that stupid mantel
looking all
good and
secret-less
are such a lie, such an awful
menacing
lie
and I am not

I cannot

I won't do it
anymore.

Betty, 1955

His name is Bill
and he is nothing like Peter

except

that he also has a car
and he also knows
where to   park it.

His name is Bill and he is different
and I am, too, with him,

except that I still say
yes
because I don't know how to say
no.   (Has anyone ever said
                                              no?)

Mom puts a photo of me
on the mantel next to her at sixteen and her mother
at sixteen
and it is a photo from
before
from my sixteenth birthday when she complained about how
lucky I was,
so I try to act like that lucky
girl on the mantel from before.

The rest of me
I just hide
here
and hope Bill
and the rest of them
never see.

And maybe I can forget it all
too.
Maybe I can
do that, I think I can, I think
the photo on the mantel
is the reminder that I
have to.

So I

do

(except
I do not. I am still
part of me
in that hospital
holding that pen
trying to find a way
across the river.)

Betty, 1955

And there it is
again,

the same feeling that is queasy and
tight,

tired and   true,

and this time when I tell Bill he says
marry me
and I say
okay
and my parents say nothing but shake their heads and stare out
the windows and later they whisper again
that I am

lucky,
so lucky,

for the way Bill will let me wear white and
buys me a ring
and wants to wear a suit with a rose pinned to the lapel.

"Almost
like a real bride,"
Mother says
with a sigh and a slump,

as if at seventeen

I am too
runed   and   wrong
to deserve nice things like
flowers
and diamonds
and Bill.

Lucky,
they say,
that someone will
have me,
even now.

And I guess they're right.
I am not like
Helen,
who is good and deserves what she has.

I am Betty
and I will never be
good
again
no matter how hard I try.

(I won't really try.)

Mimi, 2022

I want to sit in a car
with Betty,
spill out secrets
like a cup that is too full
in hands that are
clumsy. I want to see what happens when our secrets
splash and splatter and
soak us all up

My fingers itch for my
phone, a place where I could say a hundred secrets
to thousands of people,
but before I hit a single key I hear their
replies in my head about who is
good and worthy and bad and broken and what it means to be
sixteen and how it is supposed to be, and I'm starting to think
they're all
wrong
because right now sixteen is

this car leaving this driveway, leaving this house and the people
in it
to drive
without knowing where I'm going, and
online I was supposed to be a girl with some
plan that the right pair of
jeans or the right
curl-taming spray could
help with. But I am in

torn-up jeans that used to belong to
Mom and
my hair is so wild, I gathered it into pigtails
that they'd tell me are only for little kids
but that feel
good and loose and easy on my neck.

What do they know,
anyway?

Mimi, 2022

I bring
Wendy
and Tiffany
and no one else.
There are no more Betty notebooks or I'd bring her too.

Outside the door are three
sleepy
reporters
waiting to see my mother,
or maybe me,
based on how they
leap to their feet and lift their cameras and point them my way,
and some eager part of me
wants to
smile
or at least angle their cameras a little above my eye line,
part my lips,
look right into their
lenses the way I know
looks best.

"Mimi? Can you comment on how your mother is doing and
if it is true that she
has been involved with
many men in the industry over the years?"

I
almost reply. Something about

how am I supposed to know and also
she is basically in her forties, so obviously she has been involved
with men, and that it's
totally irrelevant and she's so upset and I almost tell them
I've read all about it and she's right and they're wrong and god if
anyone would just
LISTEN

but.

Instead I
breathe and then
one leans toward me
with a smile on his face like it is so
exciting
to catch me off guard. He is holding,
of course,
his phone, and on it a photo
of my mother
in tall red boots and a short black dress and her arms around
two different men,
and he asks for a comment.

The boots are
great
and the dress is
the kind I would add fabric to the bottom of, a collar to the top,
except I am
tired
of the time it takes to stitch things up, to make them
better,
all for someone who isn't even
me.
So I say,

"She looks
happy," and I
give them the finger,

which is probably a
mistake too. But
it feels

good

to look at that person in those red boots and that short dress
and say,
yes,
this is
right;
this is
a person she can
be.

And it also feels good
to jab my middle finger up to the sky,
because that is the truth
too.

Mimi, 2022

I don't know what else to do.
Buy red boots,
maybe?
Rip my clothes up so that they cover less of me
or find a sweater so that I can be
cozier
or just
keep driving?

Because what I really want is
my heart to

s   l   o   w
and
to be less alone in these ripped jeans and this old
Kamala Harris T-shirt.
So I drive to the church parking lot
and climb into my back seat
like it is my new
living room,
like it is now
where I live.

And I read.

Wendy, 1971
Sixteen, Part 2

There are people
obviously
who I could call up to
do something
on my birthday
but we'd have to talk about
like
how Dan's doing with a bad
draft number
and how I'm doing with how Dan's doing
and maybe we'd talk about the
president
or
like
some sort of new musician who sounds croaky
and sad
and I don't care much about musicians
or guitars
or presidents.

I do care about Dan
but like
right now
I want to enjoy this stolen bottle of wine
and the way it feels to say a sort of
fuck you
to Mom and her secrets hidden in the cabinet
that aren't secret at all

because when you are
that
drunk
everyone
can
tell.

There are other secrets
too
in boxes in the attic,
notebooks like this one
except belonging to Mom and Grandmother and
whoever else, I guess, had things to say but no one to say them
to.

It sounds like
a silly story from a fairy tale
about birthdays and destiny and locked attics and the girls
trapped inside.
So I have never looked in those boxes,
I have never wanted to look
at the twisted-up histories hidden in there.

Because I guess
it seems like secrets are secrets
for a reason—

the booze in Mom's
special cabinet,
the notebooks with their
stories,
and all the things banging around our
hearts,
like how I'm not even sure I want to be the girlfriend

of a guy
with a bad draft number,
which must mean I am
a very bad sort of person.
And who wants to know
a secret like that?

Some things
need to never be said
or read
or probably even
written down like this.

Mimi, 2022

I hold the notebook to my
chest and
squeeze. My body has been
b u z z i n g
for days but with my eyes closed and the notebook on my chest
it
turns from a buzz to a hum
and that hum is
easier, smaller, softer.

It was, whatever,
fifty years ago or something,
but Wendy and I are the same sort of
terrible person
who wants to know why they are terrible

and

the same secrets
maybe
made us this way.

There are a bunch of her notebooks tucked into the back seat
and even more of hers and Mom's locked in the
trunk
and I could spend the afternoon reading in this church parking
lot,
worrying about reporters finding me and asking me questions
I can't possibly answer,

or
I could go to her home,
the one with vines
crawling all over it—
the way histories crisscross and tangle up in
knots, the way our
destinies grow all over each other,
untamed and
a little bit beautiful.

I remember
the way there.

I remember
so much about the few weeks before quarantine,
what we ate and
how the air
felt
and who we saw
and what we said to them. I remember
because we replayed it,
talked through it
constantly in those early months

"Do you remember
driving along the highway
on the way to Grandma's,
stopping for burgers and fries,
eating them,
stuffed next to all those people in that shitty,
dirty
rest stop? Do you remember
getting out to look at the view
from the river

a mile away,
and how it all felt so
so
so
regular? How people just
walked around
with uncovered faces,
not knowing what was
coming? Do you remember the wrong turn we
took
and the guy
fixing that fence
who helped us—
do you think he
was the last stranger we've spoken to? Do you think he
is the last stranger we will ever speak to?" I
asked
over and
over in April and May
until Eric sighed
and left the room, mumbling about
how much I
talk,
and Mom

followed him,

of course,

always trailing behind him and never
staying with me.

Now
I just

think those same memories
silently,
still wanting to talk about those days in March, but knowing
there isn't really
room for that.

It is strange to drive the road on my own
almost three years later, my body remembering things my mind
forgets. I make the same
wrong turn
near the end
and look for the guy
fixing the fence,
wanting
somehow
to go back to those days that were simpler—

or

no

not simpler. But that *felt* simpler. The virus was
floating around us, but we didn't
know,
and whatever happened to Mom
had happened to Mom
just the same,
but she hadn't told anyone,
and no one had
yet
taken a photo
of me in a red bra

and shared it with their best friend and theirs and theirs

until someone's mom saw and
told my mom,
who told
me.

But I had the bra on
that day
and the photo was a day later
and all these things were
there
but
hidden. We felt
safe but we

weren't.

Still,
I'd like to see that fence guy
in his flannel shirt and wool hat
and be the girl I was
that day
when everything

seemed

okay.

Mimi, 2022

Her house is
there
of course,
but somehow it's a surprise that it looks so much
the same. The vines even making identical
patterns crawling across its surface
as they did back then.

It's taken all these hours of driving to realize how
actually extremely
fucked-up it is
that I'm here.

Surely
she has been watching the news. Surely
she knows what is happening with Mom and me and surely
she doesn't want to be
involved.
Because if she
cared
she would have
called. She would have
emailed or, I don't know,
shouldn't she be the one showing up at *our* door,
now that I think about it? Isn't that what mothers or
grandmothers do
when things are bad? Don't they
bring casseroles and
like

milkshakes
and tuck you in and tell you it's okay, everything will be okay?
Or maybe they
yell at the reporters and tell them to
mind their business or
something?
Anything?
Don't they even maybe
call just to yell at you
for the mistakes you've made
and let it all explode in some sky-shattering
fight that leaves you feeling wrung-out but also
somehow
steady?

What do I know,
though? I only know
what the notebooks tell me,
I guess,
and they don't say anything about
milkshakes or kind words or
even
enormous fights.

That's not our family.
Our family is
everything painful, stored in a box that you look at

alone.

Wendy, 1971

"Is love about pretending?" I ask Dan.
He is
eating ice cream
and I am
watching him eat ice cream
and thinking about the way I love or don't love
my family
and the way they love or fail to love
me.

"I hope not," Dan says. "Something you want to tell me?"
There isn't. There are just the hours I spent
in the attic
reading about
the other Wendy. The one my mother
actually wanted.
When I was reading, I kept deciding to run away, because I just
couldn't
take the way she wanted that girl and not me,
and I didn't know what to do with how I felt bad for her
and hated her too. But instead of running away I
lay on the attic floor
and closed my eyes, and then I'd
get back up and keep reading.

But now there's this little bow of
hate
around my heart
and I don't know if it's for my grandmother

my mother
that other Wendy

or me. I just know it's tied up all tight and
shiny and I never liked
bows and the way they squeeze and pull and try to make neat
and tidy what is meant to be
messy.

I am not supposed to hate
anyone in the secret story stored in the attic. But
hate is what I do
I guess
when I don't know what else
to feel.

And none of this is the kind of thing you tell someone
when a war is raging and they are
probably joining it.

"So what do you think love is about, then?" I ask.
I am pretty sure it is, in fact, about pretending. Pretending the
things that are happening
aren't.
Pretending you are fine or happy or unworried
about things like wars or drinking or
sex.
Pretending to be right here and now when part of your brain is
there and then.

"This," Dan says. "These moments here."
He is a romantic,
my Dan,
and I am
not.
"It's just this feeling,
you know? It's the best feeling in the world and wanting to
make someone happy
and being all,
you know,
happy
inside.
Right?"

Sometimes Dan speaks like he is dictating a
love note, and I never much liked his
love notes.
They seem sort of
flimsy
or silly
lately.

Love does too.
Even Dan does, some days.

I do too.

But I pretend
I feel just fine.

Wendy, 1971

"You are just fine," Mom says
when I tell her I am   scared
of the things on television

"You are right here," she says.
But I am not
really
and she is not
either

and soon, very soon, a lot of boys,
ones we know,
will be not
okay
at all.

Boys
like
Dan.

Wendy, 1971

We are watching television when we find out
that he is

going

there

and I gasp.

It is a loud gasp,
the kind that comes with gurgle and snort and cough.

"Wendy," Mom says, like the sound is
not ladylike enough.
The other Wendy is probably never making
noises or
having

feelings. The other Wendy is probably,
like,
knitting mittens for soldiers or
something. She is probably smiling very sweetly and,
I don't know,
praying.

I am not that Wendy, though. I am
this one.

That bow of hate
around my heart
tightens.

"That's Dan's number," I say.
Mom nods
only once
and gets up
to go to the kitchen
to make chicken
that tastes like salt and nothing else,

and she asks me to turn off the television and eat it,
the salty chicken,
and I say no, I'm not eating, I'm not pretending this isn't
happening.
The other Wendy would have eaten the chicken. The other
Wendy
would have
made the chicken.

Mom eats by herself at the dining room table
and maybe she makes conversation
with,
like,
dinner rolls
or
candlesticks,

but I can't hear anything at all
from this space I am hiding inside,
the space where I know he is going to leave and
not

come
back.

Wendy, 1971

Dan orders us grilled cheese
and he has a straight
            straight
            back.

"It's an honor," he says,
which is a lie,
but he likes the way it looks on him,
the way it makes him
seem
older and wiser and better.

The other Wendy would probably want to date someone so
solid,
so good.

I itch with the knowledge that I can only
unfortunately
be this Wendy.

Mimi, 2022

That is the Wendy
I want to know. The one who
doesn't love who she should.

I laid on the ground,
too,
when I was reading Betty's notebooks.

I worry,
too,
about my heart and what is
tied around it, what is
making it hard to

breathe.

Still I do my best to

breathe.

And get out of the car.
And knock on her door.

Mimi, 2022

My grandmother,
who I've only met once,
doesn't look surprised to
see me.
"The famous Mimi," she says. "Daughter of the even more
famous
Tiffany
Dovewick."
She

sighs.

I don't know how,
but until right now I hadn't realized
that if Walter Bruce did something
to my mom,
my grandmother
probably
should have known.

Mimi, 2022

"I didn't know where else to go,"
I say.
"So here you are," my grandmother says,
opening the door,
motioning me
in.

We barely know each other, except also
I know her better than I know
most people
just from her notebooks,
from the way she said she is
unwanted and hard to love,
from the way she said she is
all kinds of wrong.

Inside it is all
floral furniture and
framed photos from long ago
and lacy curtains that don't keep out the sun.

"She hates me," I say, because I drove all the way here,
so I might as well say something
real.

"No," my grandmother says, and I think I can see
Wendy somewhere in there,
behind wrinkles and her wry smile.
"She hates herself."

My grandmother says it like she has hated herself
too. And I know she
has. I almost ask about the bow of hate and if it ever
comes undone.
But I don't.

We eat
strawberries
and turkey sandwiches,
and we talk about
not much
until we talk about
everything.

"She never told me," my grandmother says about
Walter Bruce. "Though I guess
I wouldn't have wanted her to. Some things
are better kept
to ourselves, Mimi."

And I know,
quicker than a breath, quicker than a blink,
that things have happened to her,
too,
not just Dan going to war
but other things, things
we don't talk about, things that maybe happen to
everyone
but we pretend happen to
no one.

"Would you have believed her?" I ask. I want to know
if I was supposed to believe my mother more easily,

if I was supposed to be a different kind of daughter.
Maybe, like my grandmother, I am also
wishing I were
Other Wendy.

Maybe that other Wendy
was the best of us, the rest of us just sad,
sorry
imitations of the one who was taken away; the rest of us
never quite making up for that
loss.

I thought it was the notebooks
haunting us,
but maybe it is actually
Other Wendy
and the better life she probably lives.
We are the
disappointments.
Sad,
secret-keeping replacements for the
daughter Betty didn't get to
keep.

I try to
swallow it down but it
just keeps living in my heart and limbs and that space below my
chest where the worst feelings
live.

"Your mom wanted to be famous," my grandmother says. "And
she
got her way,
didn't she?"

She brings out tea and cookies, like we are in
England or something,
like we are refined and elegant. I try to sit with a straight back
and
crossed legs. I don't know the rules
here
or if they are different from Mom's
rules. I hope I am wearing the right clothes; I hope I look
like a granddaughter.

"Your mom kept things from you
too," I say. "Obviously. Big things. Huge secrets.
What did you—I mean how did you—what do I do
now? How do I—
I want it to be simpler."

My grandmother,
who is also Wendy,
and who is also not
that same Wendy
anymore,

                                        smiles.

"They're not secrets" she says. "We say what we need to say. We
write it down.
It's all there. In the notebooks. This is where things are
safe,
Mimi. You and your
generation, you want it all
up there
online,
but the important things,
we hold on to them, we write them down.

And that is
family. That's our family."

She sounds so sure
that a notebook is enough.
But the notebooks are
flimsy and water-stained and hard to read
sometimes and
they
always stop after a year or so. They do not cover
decades of our lives;
they don't house
all the secrets that make us
who we are. The notebooks are
one moment in time but they aren't
everything.

I need to know more
than the one moment in time I got to know about her
or Mom
or me.

"Where have you been
all these years?" I ask,
the words coming out faster,
stronger,
than I thought they would, a waterfall that I thought would be a
dripping faucet. A hurricane that I meant to be
a breeze.
"Why is it this way? Why has it always been me and Mom
and no one else
except these stupid guys
who aren't even my dad? Why haven't we had
you

or him
or Betty or anyone else?
Are we just meant to be
alone? Meant to be quiet, meant to only know what we read
in an attic?
Why are we so   untethered?

"This is our family," my grandmother says.
She says it
with force,
her own little hurricane. "This is our
destiny or
our place, our way of
being and surviving and
moving forward. Not every family is
the same, Mimi."

She keeps saying my name, like it will make me
feel the same things she feels, make me believe in her idea
of what our family has to be. Who mothers and daughters and
grandmothers and
great
great
great
grandmothers
have to be to each other.

But my name sounds all
fresh and timid in her mouth.
A word she's
basically never said
and is trying out for the first time.

"I'm asking why," I say. "Why does it have to be

this way? You could come over. You could call or tell us
who you are or
how you feel about who we are
or
anything. We could say the things out loud
that we write down. Couldn't we? Couldn't you?"

She starts
clearing plates and making herself
busy.

"It's tradition," she says,
as if leaving your family behind is
the same as making apple pie from scratch,
playing Trivial Pursuit with your cousins at the family reunion,
having breakfast for dinner on your birthday,
taking a first-day-of-school photo on the front steps,
writing in a notebook
during your sixteenth year.

She says it
like leaving is a kind of magic,
a kind of
curse,
something inevitable and built into a
Once Upon a Time,
like we are the story of a family
and not an actual family.

"Couldn't we choose to make it not
tradition?" I ask,
and I feel myself leaning in her direction,
wanting her to say something
that grandmothers say,

wanting her to make it different.

Maybe
she knows who my father is or where Betty's other
daughter lives. Maybe she knows
what happened to Mom and whose fault it was. Maybe
she even
has a map of the way forward,
maybe she will transform
right now, before my eyes, into a
Matriarch
who holds court over Thanksgiving dinners, telling us how to
carve a turkey
fold a napkin
say a prayer
be a family.

But that's
I guess
not how destiny
works.

"It's silly," she says, "to fight so hard against the way things
are. You see that, with what your mom is
doing. It's
silly to try to make a big
scene
about men and girls with bodies like ours
and how you wish it was,
instead of just
accepting
how it is. It's easier,
isn't it,
to just

let it be."

Mimi, 2022

I think I thought
exactly that

before.

I wanted the past
in the boxes in the attic, Mom's history,
locked away,

and that would maybe mean mine could one day be
locked away
too.

But.

My grandmother lives in this house
covered in vines, remembering or not remembering a boy
named
Dan, and there is a whole story in her notebooks
that I know I need to read,
not because it is
destiny

but because it is
a map
of the way things have been,
which is maybe also
a map of the way
things don't have to be

anymore.

Mimi, 2022

We don't hug goodbye
at the door.

She doesn't send me home with
cookies
or anything.

"The past is the past," she says with a certainty that I never
feel about anything.
"But it isn't
really," I say
to her back as she turns away,
because,
I mean,
the past is also
sitting in the back seat of my car,
and it is also
being talked about on CNN,
and it is also
the reason I don't wear red lace bras
anymore,
and it is also
somewhere
out there,
making a present
of its own.

Wendy, 1971
The Party, Part 1

Dan's mother throws the party
months later, when Dan is back from
training,
right before he leaves
for Vietnam.
After training he is
a little more
broad-shouldered, a little less
talkative.

After training I am
a little less comfortable in heels and I'm trying something
new
with my hair
and
I am
tired of being asked how Dan is
when I never know the answer and can only really answer
how I am,
not that they ever ask

that.

The party is
what a party for Dan's mother
might be,

even though the party is
supposedly
for Dan.

It is
sparkling
everything,
and too-sweet cake,
and Dan's uncle who is also named
Dan
taking shots
in the hallway
where he thinks no one can see him,

but I can see him.
I have a nose for
people keeping secrets,
especially if they are doing it

poorly.

It is our friend Alexandra
who can't stop crying,
blubbering, really,
and who   snot-faced   tries to kiss Dan on
the
mouth,
because Alexandra is that certain type of
girl
who wants to have kissed someone
tragic.
       (Last year she let Martin touch her breasts

when she found out his mom had died.)

Dan and I hold hands and talk to people we don't want to talk
to,
but still
still!
It is better than talking about
the War.

Dan's father pulls me aside.
He smells like beer   we all do
        and chips   that too
and we listen to Elton John's "Your Song"
for a moment;
then he asks me,
"Will you wait for him?" and before I answer,
he turns it into a statement.

"You'll wait for him, Wendy.
It will keep him
alive.
He needs someone to
come
home
to."

And like that—faster than Elton can finish
telling me how wonderful life is
now that I'm in the world—
I become
a fixed object.
Someone not allowed to be anyone but
this
girl

right
now
in a blue dress
with a tall boyfriend
who is polite to strangers.

I'd thought maybe I would
join a band or
go to college or
go to bed with someone
not drafted into a war I don't understand,
but

no.

Dan's father   wearing a Mickey Mouse tie all wrong for the
occasion
tells me I will not do anything
but
wait.

Dan's grandmother—young enough to be his mother and
so
sugar-sweet—
says Dan needs a girl like
me,
and it's funny, because how does she know
who I am,
when I
do not?

Wendy, 1971
The Party, Part 2

"Will you be waiting for him?"
Dan's father asks, again, while we dance to something slow.

I did not say I'd like to dance
with Dan's father,
who looks like Dan but with
a beer belly and
a smoker's cough and
hands that sit too squarely on my
hips.

"You will," he answers for me. I do not
like that I can feel the words on my
neck through beer-brimmed breath.

I catch Dan's eye across the room—
he's dancing with his mother,
who is in a purple satin cocktail dress and
wobbly heels,
like it is our wedding reception
and not
the weekend before he leaves for
war.
She has her arms around his neck,
a place where my arms usually
live,
and she heaves sobs

against him.

"He needs to know you're just right here," Dan's father says—
different words saying the same things
he's already said.
I'd never noticed his Southern twang
or the hairiness of his knuckles.
I've never noticed that he thinks I am a person
who exists only
in relation to Dan,
a person to write home to; a person to miss
vaguely and without worry
about what they had for lunch
or who they think they may want to
become.

"What he really needs is the president to end the war," I say.
I don't remember enough of Government Studies
to know if presidents can stop wars
or stop this one
now
but I say it anyway because maybe
it will surprise Dan's father's hands
away from my ass,
where he is letting one
solitary
thumb
wander.

"Boys die over there," Dan's father says,   (as if I never
said a word about presidents)
"if they don't think there's a reason to come home. A beautiful
reason."
It is a threat.

So is his thumb;
so is this song that is lasting forever;
so is Dan's sobbing mother and how she keeps
sobbing.

They all want me to stay right here,
waiting,
which is so, so different   it turns out
than

being.

Wendy, 1971
At the Party Where There Are Some Things About This Moment That I Cannot Seem to Stop

The other Wendy
would know how to stop

this.

Or. No.
The other Wendy
is surely not the kind of girl who
lets this sort of thing happen
at all.

She probably
wears pink and pearls and everyone knows
not to touch her,
not to

touch any part of her.

Things like this
happen to Wendys like me
who sway their hips to songs and like short skirts and

say
somehow
with our smiles

sure, okay,
I won't tell anyone.

People can tell
just by looking at me
that I know about secrets. Keeping them and
being them
too.

Wendy, 1971
The Party, Part 3
A Closer Look at What Is Happening Here and Now

Dan's father's thumb
has found the top line of my
underwear,
which is white,
but Dan's father's thumb doesn't know the color.

I hope.

> *(I should say something*
> *about his thumb but*
> *it's*

> *embarrassing. The way it*
> *lingers like I'm fine with it and*
> *he probably thinks I am fine with it*
> *because*
> *it's been fifteen seconds and then thirty and*
> *I've said nothing, I should have said*
> *something the moment it happened*
> *and now it's too late and*
> *Dan really loves*
> *his dad, who maybe*
> *doesn't know where his thumb is or would*
> *know if he was sober but he isn't because*

none of us are because Dan is going to war.
And a good, kind girl,
like Other Wendy, would, I'm sure,
just be
nice, and I need to be
nice because he is grief-stricken and I am
here.)

Dan's father's thumb is acting all casual,
as if the top of my ass is
a place it's meant to
be.
But my legs are tight
and I've lost the rhythm of the
song
and I wish I'd worn something else
or I wish I wasn't here at all

(I'm grief-stricken, too,
though,
and my thumb is
on his arm, where thumbs are
meant to be, and I almost say
something, except if I say it, it will
come out as a yell or a scream or
a hard shove, and I can't
turn this party into the party
where I screamed at Dan's dad
before Dan went to war to deal with
real things. I can't. I can't.
He could just
GOD
Couldn't he just

stop when he feels me jerk

away,
when he sees my red face
when he hears my tiny, tiny voice say
"um,
excuse me?"
and nothing else?)

as Dan's father's thumb
slides back and forth
and makes itself known
and I shift my hips
to try to make it lose
its way.

Wendy, 1971

It's not like I can tell
Dan.

What matters is that he is going to war,
and it does not matter
what his father's thumb did
or did not
do.

I tuck the moment away
and become the girl they all want me to be,
a girl who

is on pause.

A girl
in a photo
tucked close to a soldier's heart.

I decide to be
only
that girl.

It's fine. It's who I'm meant to be:
a girl who looks nice
because no one can see
her secrets.

Mom says, without saying it exactly, that that's who we are
meant to be anyway.

Wendy, 1971

It's not like Dan and I ever shared a bed.
We weren't,
like,
married
or whatever.

But still.

There is an emptiness to my bed,
that he was never actually in,
and I keep thinking of things I'd like to tell him.

That they started rebuilding the library
and
that I ate a perfect avocado.
That I dreamt about roses that knew how to
sing,
that I finished that book I didn't think I was going to finish,
that when the news comes on at night my mother
finds a way to usher me out of the room,
which is
I guess meant to be
kind?
but actually makes me feel sort of

invisible.

I want to tell him what his Dad
did
and how I want to be wrong about it but that I'm
actually
pretty sure that I'm

not?

I want to tell him I do not like
being
a girl in a photo, because actually
I'm also
right here.

But.
That won't save his life. So.

I write
I love you so much
on stationery with pink flowers
that I got for some birthday
a hundred years ago
when I was the kind of girl who someone thought might like to
write
letters on
pink-flowered stationery.

And I guess they were
sort of

right?

Wendy, 1971

I wait
and wait
and

wait.

The postman
comes at the same time every day,
which is right when I get home from school,
and we do a sort of dance
where he bows his head and cringes
and I lead with my heart and hope there is an envelope
smothered with stamps
from Vietnam.

Somehow this postman
sees me. And only with him I am someone other than
the girl in the photo
tucked next to Dan's heart.

He notices my haircut
and what book I'm holding
and whether my mom is
awake
or not
at three thirty in the afternoon.

"She's in a bad way today?" he'll say,
and Mom would hate it
because it's sort of against the rules
to say something so obvious and true,
but the postman says stuff like that.
The kind of things Mom and I only
say in our notebooks,
where it's safe.

"Sometimes it takes a whole hell of a long time,
letters coming from over there to here. I've seen it all.
It can take a long time," he says
when it has been
too long
and no letters have
come.
"It's already been a long time," I say.

And we both think the same thoughts,
and I know he is rooting for me
and for Dan
and for all the things that we both know are about to not
come
true.

Wendy, 1971

When they come to tell Dan's family
three doors down,
it is 3:27
in the afternoon
on a Saturday
and Mom is in a bad way
and the postman is heading to our house
and we see them at the same time,
the postman and I.

Men in their uniforms.
They take off their hats
when Dan's mom answers the door.
And I collapse
into the postman's
wobbly arms.

Wendy, 1971
Things About Dan I'd Rather Not Know
but Do in Fact Know

What time he died, exactly,
and who was there.

What he said at the end,
which was my name, Wendy.

And how that means,
apparently,
according to,
like,
everyone,
I can't ever love anyone
else.

It means,
apparently,
I will be the girl in the photo
forever. The love of someone
who died in war,
and that's

it.

Mimi, 2022

My car is
hot,
unbelievably hot, even though it's winter,
and outside it is starting to snow, but
inside this car it is
hot and I am hot and I am
cramped and my legs want to move, all of me wants to
m   o   v   e.

I want to go back to my grandmother's house and tell her
I get it, I get it, you are this way and my mom is this way and me,
too,
I am this way, too, but we don't have to be
we don't
we don't
we could be
someone else, couldn't we?
And we'll probably never meet
Other Wendy, and who knows if she's
so perfect anyway
and
my great-
great-grandmother or whatever
was a silent film star
but that doesn't mean we have to be
silent
film
stars, all faces making
expressions and lips moving

but nothing coming

out.

*You don't have to be the girl in the photo
anymore!* I want to say, but she is
decades later
somehow
still
the girl in the photo

and I am
also
I realize
still
three years later
the girl in the photo
with a red bra and a beckoning
tongue,
and Mom is
also
a girl
in a photo,
looking like a sexy fairy and

I mean

fuck

        (I kick my feet and it hurts my toes.
        I open the windows of the car
        but don't feel any less

trapped.)

we should get to be
people
roaming the world
making new mistakes,
having new
triumphs,
and we should not have to be
girls in photos

anymore.

And maybe Mom looks weird on some girl's T-shirt,
but still she is saying
I am not that girl in that photo that you think I am,
or *I* am *that girl,*
but it doesn't mean
what you think it does.

        (I open the windows wider and cold air
        pours in, hits my face, makes my eyes
        water.)

Me too, maybe.
Maybe I am that girl in the red lace bra
because, I mean,
I am,
I am that girl, that happened to me, it was a moment that
happened
to me,

but maybe
being that girl in that photo
doesn't mean
what everyone keeps on telling me
it means.

Mimi, 2022

I am buzzing
when I get home. Buzzing and sure,
which is maybe something I have never felt
before.

"Mimi, Jesus Christ, where have you been?" Eric greets me. He
is
sweating;
he is running his hands through his graying hair.
"Your mom is—
she's looking for those
notebooks
and they're not there,
thank god,
because she wants to
read them to some
ridiculous
reporter. She wants—
I don't even know what this woman is
doing,
but you need to stop her."

Eric has a photograph, too,
of Mom
from the night they met. I've seen him pull out his phone
and show it to people,
like she is some prize he has won.
In the photo she is
laughing and her shirt

sparkles and his arms wrap around her
in this loose, silly way,
and she leans her head back
so that they are touching at every possible point.

She's beautiful
there,
but it's not a version of my mother that I see

often. It is not the

truest part of her.

I'm not going to stop my mother
from anything, I think,
but do not tell
this man who thinks he knows
but does not understand
who
we
are.

"Where is she?" I ask instead,
and he points
to the attic.

Mimi, 2022

We haven't been up here together
recently,
not since long before she gave me a notebook of my own and
told me to read hers.

The attic is a part of our home but also feels
somehow
like another world entirely—
the quality of light so dusty and muted;
the heat from the house not quite reaching this

                         far corner.

Up here we can be   different versions of
                           ourselves from
                               the ones from the
                           notebooks.

"Mom. I have them," I say to stop the way her body is
shaking and frantic,
tearing tutus and bathing suits and bathrobes and doll clothes
and sweat-stained pillowcases
out of boxes,
the whole space now a sea of
cotton and tulle and spandex and fleece—an ocean of the things
you should throw away
but can't quite bring yourself to.
"I have your notebooks. And Wendy's. All of them. It's
fine. They're
safe."

I think I mean to say that
she is safe.
It's a thing I want to be true,
but that doesn't make it
true.

Mom looks at me like I am
another ghost in the attic.

"I thought the notebooks had to be secret," she says.
"That the truth had to be
just for us. But Mimi,
I wrote it all down the way it felt when it happened,
and Mimi. There's
someone else."
"What does that mean?" We are both fluttering and flying and
frantic
and I want us to find each other amid all this frenzied flapping.
"Another girl. There's another girl."
Mom's
crying
and it's sudden and it's
ugly and heaving and so big I want to make it stop but
I don't, I let it
go.
"Another girl came forward. Used her name. Another girl. She
said
it happened to her, too, and she said
she believed me and she said
she remembers me and
she said I was the kind of person who remembers
everything
because I was always carrying around
a notebook,

writing everything down. She said it was
annoying,
like I was some goody two-shoes, some
kiss-ass actress, but she said
it happened to her, too, and that kiss-ass actresses
remember things
the way they happened."

Mom looks at me and her eyes are all
blue-green-brown, this shade no one can ever really
settle on,
and her eyes are asking me
if she really might be
not a sexy-fairy-wood-nymph-failed-actress Mom but actually
a kiss-ass with a notebook
who people
believe.

"It's in the notebooks, Mimi. And it's not
perfect, it's not the story of someone saying
the clearest sort of
no, and
Eric said the truth made me look—" She shakes her head.
She takes a breath big enough for both of us.
"But the truth is
a fucking gift,
Mimi. Betty's first daughter, she doesn't
have it. And that other woman who came forward, she doesn't
have it,
not like this, not in black-and-white, written down on the page,
not crisp and clear and real. And even if the truth is
that I liked him
liking me, liked that I might be
a beautiful, wantable actress,

the truth is also
that I was too young and he was
wrong."

She looks up to the wooden beams that hold up
the attic
the house
our lives.
They look flimsy,
like they are mostly for show, and I guess the things that are
essential don't always look
sturdy and strong and
together. I guess we don't know exactly what's
holding us together
after all.

Mom takes a deep   breath.
    "Maybe you liked,"   she says,
"the way beer tasted
and how it felt to have boys
    look at you   in that way.
And maybe you liked
having a red bra and feeling   beautiful.
    Maybe you liked them   liking you,
but you were

young. And they were

wrong. And you

need to know that."

She looks

exhausted. Like she's run a marathon, like she's used everything
she has
to get that out,
and that makes sense,
actually,
because I am tired that way, too,
from finally understanding
who is at fault and who is

not.

Mimi, 2022

There is a notebook open on the floor,
and it is not mine
or Mom's or Wendy's or Betty's.
It is from further back,
a life I don't know at all.

"Were you reading this?" I ask Mom.
"No, were you?"
I shake my head. "Ghosts," I say.
"Our ghosts," Mom says, and we
lean in,
our heads touching,
our breathing
finally
in and out
at the same time,
and we

read.

Virginia, 1924

On-screen they tell me I look
luminous.
That is what they say,
so it must be true.

They think I am
twenty
on my sixteenth birthday.

Because how can I be sixteen when
the studio men
comment on my
lips
and also my
waist
and also know my
hotel room number
because they bought it for me?

This is what Mother was desiring, though,
when she brought my photograph to these
men in suits who smelled like
liquor and cigars and other vices too.
This is certainly what Mother wanted
when she put us in matching
dresses
and taught me how to smoke a cigarette
and how to lean forward when talking to a
man.

"This is how you become
a star," she said, and I think she
knew
that it would not look
quite as glamorous as it looks
on-screen.

Still, she wanted me to be
seen,
so I must do what they tell me to do,
I think, when one or another of them
visits the hotel room
late at night. *This is what*
Mother wanted, I think,
trying to unhear the sound of their
zippers
grunts
apologies.

"She will be great
in films," they say
during the day,
like I had passed some
test
the night
before.

And this is what it means to be
a glamorous
Hollywood
film
star.

I'm a star,
I tell myself as they move my body around the world
and tell it what to do. *I'm a star,*
I tell myself when I watch them
watching me
on-screen, so certain the shape of my lips and the
slope, slide, slip of my body
tells them
who
I
am.

Mimi, 2022

"I hadn't read that one before," Mom says.
"Me neither. It's
awful; it started all the way back
then and brought us
here and we are so
trapped."

But Mom shakes her head.
"No. No, listen, Mimi.
I hadn't read
a lot of the notebooks. I wasn't—

I couldn't. I thought it was just
me,
just something about
who I was that made him
do it. I didn't know—
I didn't—
It wasn't . . .
The woman who came forward,
the other one,
Stephanie. Her name is
Stephanie
and she's a doctor now. She—
I remember her—she
wore glasses and was so
skinny,

so narrow and lanky and not at all
like us.
And he did it to
her too. He—
It wasn't—
I wasn't—
and you weren't
either. Destiny isn't always
destiny, and we aren't
cursed
any more than everyone is
cursed,
and Mimi,
the notebooks aren't a promise of what has to happen,
after all. I don't know what they are, but they aren't
that."

The sentences won't come out all
full and pretty and correct. It is just the
beginnings of thoughts and the way they trail off.
It is the beginning of understanding something; it is
the way it takes time
to know something
fully;
it is the way
strangers and ghosts and
mothers and daughters
are all trying to figure it out
together.

"I wanted it to be different
for you. But there was that
photo.
And then you

turned sixteen and it wasn't different
and the things people said on your
photos online and
I just thought—"

Mom shakes her head like she saw the photo for the first time
yesterday,
like it is still
happening right now,
and I guess in some ways
it is.

I thought I turned sixteen and she just really
hated the way it hung on me;
I thought I turned sixteen and she stopped caring about anyone
but
herself,
but
oh,
wow,
no. I turned sixteen and she
wanted to change
the world
for me
but just didn't

know how.

Mimi, 2022

"That girl.
Stephanie.
She's right. It's all
written down. It's all—
I have it all." Mom looks
nervous
but also
sure.

Mom looks out the window of the attic at the
mess of reporters below:
their cameras
their casual conversations about nothing while they loiter on our
lawn
their occasional calls up to us
their taking notes and answering emails and
waiting for our story to become

theirs.

"I went to see your mom," I say. I have to say it
before anything else around us shifts.
"My mother?" Mom
inhales. Holds it in. Closes her eyes.

"Yes."

She exhales.
Sometimes
when I think of my mother,
I have to hold my breath too. Sometimes I need a moment
before

e
x
h
a
l
i
n
g.

"What did she say?" Mom asks. And I see the
w   a   n   t   i   n   g
on her face. The wanting for something to be
fixed or said or unsaid or accepted.
Something to have been stitched up and made better and
solved.

"She said this is our
destiny
or something," I say. "Or our curse, I guess. That this is just
who we are, this is how we have to
live,
with secrets and shame and
notebooks and whatever. But you're saying now that that's
not right? That that doesn't have to be
right?"

Now it is my face
that I'm sure is filled with
wanting.

In some families
a middle name is passed down,
a set of china,
a love of
horses or gardens or books or baseball.

What I want to know
is
if this body,
passed down through generations,
means a certain fate, a way things have to go. Because that's kind
of
how it seems. That we didn't get horses or baseball or fancy
china or
a green thumb. We got a body that somehow belongs to
everyone else,
a body that gives
permission, a body that
asks to be
mistreated.

What I want to know is,
can I ask for something better than this body and the secrets
it is told it has to keep?

"*No,* Mimi," Mom says. She puts an arm around me.
She pulls me
in.
"No. This is not
how it has to be."

She grabs the notebooks from 1999 and we
go downstairs, where Eric is

fuming on the couch,
saying something about everybody needing to
calm down,
take a step back,
think,
but I don't care what he says,
I am going for the mantel,
for the photos
all lined up and matching and telling us who we are. Looking all
inevitable.
We have put them on display and hid
the truth up in the attic
for ages,
and
that's not how it's going to be
anymore.

I pile them up in my arms
and bring them outside,
where Mom is flipping through notebooks
and reporters are snapping photos.
"Girls in photos
on a mantel
can't do anything," I say. "Girls in photos
on a mantel
are trapped
in silent,
unmoving
films. You know?
Mom, you know what I mean?"

And she does.

Mimi, 2022

They go in
the trash. I don't
shatter them or anything so
dramatic. I just
throw them
away.

Probably
reporters are watching and snapping photos
of me, new ones that say something else
about who I am,
but I
don't adjust the way my body is angled toward them, and I don't
check what I'm wearing or
wonder what they think of it. I just
throw
the photos
from the mantel
away
and let that be
the whole story.

"God, it feels good,
actually,
to be rid of
them," Mom says,
shaking out her arms,
leaning her head back and forth like the photos
from the mantel

had been
affixed to her for many long and painful
years.

It's impossible,
actually,
to be what a photograph insists on. Photographs
are still and
fixed and are a vision of a girl
from one angle
in one particular kind of light
on one day with one
thought
running through her mind.

We

move in and out of
different patches of light.

We are

different during a noon rainstorm than we might be
at midnight or
just before dawn

or as the sun begins to disappear,
like it is doing now,
throwing shadows
all around us.

Mimi, 2022

On instinct I want to post a picture of
this,
too,
like the realization isn't real if it isn't
in a photo
online
for everyone to see.

So I
log on
and see the last photo I posted, which was
me at Christmas, and the comment section is now just a
parade of hate
about what a terrible daughter I am,
how desperate I am for fame,
and how girls like me don't have friends because we don't
deserve them. The names commenting are mostly
strangers,
but not all. There are people from school,
saying
yes
you are right
she is
bad, she is that
bad kind of girl
who ruins
everything.

I wonder what it is I've

ruined,
sitting in the back of AP History, taking notes on a war that
Wendy lost her
love in;
talking about the Super Bowl commercials in the cafeteria with
people who don't know anything
about me;
hanging in the back of a dance
that Mom makes me go to
that no one really wants me at,
at least,
that's how it feels based on the way they look at my dress,
the comments they make about
the way it
fits.

What,
from the collection of tiny
tragedies that is
high school
for me,
do they hate
so
much?

I scroll more through the strangers' comments
until I see one name
Clinton Dover
and my heart
jump-skips,
cartwheels,
loses its place in my body,
and I brace myself
for the terrible things he'll tell them about me

and how impossible I am to
love
or even
like a little.

But
instead he's written:

She's—
like everyone else—
a little bit of this person
here
in these photos
and a lot of someone else
entirely
who just wants to
I don't know
be okay. Maybe we should let her
try
to be
okay without all these
comments about the ways she
isn't
okay.

She's—
she hates parties and she loves
fuzzy socks and she's very
polite with parents and she's
funny
she says these surprising
funny
things
and when she's sad she

lashes out
but mostly at herself
and she likes to drink coffee
alone
at a coffee shop where they know her order
and they draw a smiley face on her lid
and she
loves
that smiley face
and
maybe those are small facts
about her
but so are these

photos. They are
small facts
too.

I think I might
stop breathing or even
stop
being.

And then
I start again:
breathing
being
believing, even, a little bit.

And I hit the heart
next to his comment and write in

just the words
thank you.

I do not
post a photo
or respond to other comments
or try to be
anything
to anyone
except
I try to be
a daughter
to my mother,
who is staring at the reporters
with a notebook in her hand
and a look on her face
I've never seen before.

Mimi, 2022

"What if I just
read it?"
Mom whispers.
The cameras are still
f   l   a   s   h   i   n   g
around us,
telling some other story
than the one happening right here
between us.

Mom is so close to me I smell her
lavender soap and the last traces of
green tea on her breath. It's been so long since we've stood
close,
so the smell is nearly unfamiliar,
except it is also so much
mine,
belonging to me.

"Read what?" I whisper back.
"The notebook. The entry about
it. About what happened
with Walter Bruce."
"Read it, like, here? Now? To them?"

I notice
all of a sudden
that I am Mom's height
exactly

now. It isn't much of an accomplishment;
she never quite reached five feet,
and I may not either,
but I have reached
her:
our shoulders hitting one another,
our noses
aligned.
I think she notices it,
too,
in the same moment,
which is this one
right here.

"I think,
maybe,
yeah,
right here and now.
I know the lawyers wouldn't—
that's not what would be
advised, I'm sure,
but it's
mine,
Mimi,
you know? It's mine and also
yours and also
all of ours,
but it's mine and right now feels—
if you don't want me to, I won't, but it's the kind of thing
I have never wanted
to do
and may never want to do
again,
so

I don't know,
what if I just
stand here
and you stand here with me
and I
read?

What if we decide
what these words
mean?"

Mimi, 2022

Mom's voice is
clear,
pretty,
and maybe she could have been a voice-over actress
or radio star
but no one ever
noticed
the lilting, lovely, bouncing vowels and crisp,
proud
consonants.

Maybe
maybe they will notice
now.

Tiffany, 1999
As Read By Tiffany, 2022

Walter Bruce's couch is as big
as a bed.

"Let's see
what you have," he says
with this
smile
like he's looking at a menu
and every dish is
his favorite.

My new headshots are in a folder
with unicorns on the front,
because all I could find was my seventh-grade
Trapper Keeper,
and it was this or
ballerina bears.

I hand it over and feel
like the same kid who loved unicorns and bears in tutus,
but I try to look like
not a kid,
like a sexy fairy,
like an actress that he wants to work with,
like the exact sort of girl he
imagined me being
when he pulled me over that day on set;
when he handed me this photographer's card;

when he told me what it is that's special about me.

He takes his time.
In the photos I am in something pink and
shimmery. My makeup,
too,
has the suggestion of sparkle, my lips parted
the way,
I guess,
fairies do. My hair looks a little like a
halo,
lit to seem more golden,
more glowing,
like I am made of moons and stars
and not flesh and blood.

In every shot there is the promise of my
breasts
and a
l   e   a   n
in my body
that makes me
uncomfortable—
it looks like I'm asking someone to
come over,
to be near me,
to look at me more
closely,
which Walter Bruce
does.

His eyes flit from the photos to me and back again. I am not in
shimmery pink
right now,

but I am in something white with
fluttery sleeves,
and I let my hair fall all around my shoulders, hanging in my
face
a little. I'd like to push it away,
but the photographer says it looks
best
like this.

"Well, well,

well," he says. "Tiffany Dovewick. That's more like it. This—
this
we can do something with. You captured it. That strange
combination of
innocent and

not. Angel and

devil. Fairy-being in the woods who we all
sort of want to

{he pauses, looking for the word}

touch."

I think
there was another word
underneath that one, a more honest word
that he chose not to
say.

He gets up from his
desk,
still holding one of my photos,
and sits next to me on the
couch, and so fast
I can't keep up,
his hand is on my thigh.
"I see
big things for you," he says. "With these photos, we can really
find a place for you. There's
demand
for this kind of girl." He pats the photo with his finger,
then lets that finger find
my breast. "That's what you want,
right?" he says. "To be this kind of
girl, this one in this photo that we're asking you to
be? You can be
her,
right?"

"Sure," I say
even though I don't know if I can or want to or
should,
but I do know that I can't say
no
to Walter Bruce.

"That's what I thought," he says, and his hand,
the one on my thigh,
inches up
and up,
and the finger on my breast swirls and,
I guess,
this is what is happening,
and so I
let it
happen.

When it is over,
I say
"no," like I've finally remembered
the answer to a question
no one asked me.

"What's that?" Walter Bruce says,
zipping his

pants, straightening his
tie.

I shake my head,
the word already

gone,

Mimi, 2022

Mom had been looking at the notebook and I had been looking at Mom,
but when she finishes, we both look

up.

The reporters are
silent and scribbling,
holding up cameras and phones.
They are all

                                                          still

for one perfect instant,
stunned and slack-jawed,
and then their hands raise
alongside their voices:

Are you saying it was
Did you say no
What happened next did you take a part in his
Why didn't you tell
What else did you write
Can anyone corroborate
What, specifically did he
Will you be releasing that
Was it a poem
How old were you exactly
Tiffany Tiffany Tiffany Tiffany
Are you
sure?

I grab Mom's
hand,
a thing I haven't done since I was too young to cross the street
on my own.
It is cold and
sweaty,
and I hope that's not
regret
that I feel on her skin, see on her scared and
quiet face.

She doesn't speak, so I give her time to see if she
will,
but nothing comes, so I
squeeze her hand once and say
in a voice that comes from who-knows-where,
"That's all
for now; that's her
statement
or whatever. No, um,
no further
comments."

And I pull Mom
inside,
where Eric is
p   a   c   i   n   g,
but otherwise things are
better than the swarm and swirl of
outside.

"Get her water," I say,

using the same voice I used with the reporters,
a stronger voice than I knew I had. "Mom, sit
down.
That was,
wow,
that was—"
"My lawyer's gonna kill me," she says. "You're never supposed to
say anything
without a lawyer, Mimi."
"That was amazing," I say. "Lawyer or not,
Mom,
that was
incredible."
She shakes her head, but I need her to hear me.
"It was—
we've had these secrets for all these years,
and there you were just
just

freeing us from them.
Just letting them
be. I mean, that's—"

"It's really fucking
stupid is what it is," Eric interrupts. "You just told them that
you didn't say
no. I mean, god, Tiff,
you said
sure. This is what I've been trying to
tell you. You don't have some

case against this guy. It's been
twenty years.
You said
sure.
You made the film.
You had
years
of contact with him after,
begging him to
hire you.
I mean,
god,
it's like you want to make life
impossible. You and
Mimi
taking things and turning them all inside out and upside
down,
writing poems
to twist up
the truth."

Eric keeps shaking his head like he just can't believe
us.
Mom
shrinks.

But Eric's words don't make me small.
Not
anymore.

"The poems don't twist up the truth," I say. "They
untwist
and untangle
and make it all

crystal clear. And if that truth feels confusing
to you,
maybe you should
leave."

Eric looks
at me and at Mom and back and forth.
I'm not sure
exactly what he's waiting for
until Mom
lets her head nod
once, lets her body
shift closer to mine, lean into mine, her hand
back in mine
again.

Mimi, 2022

They
hate us and love us and think we are
heroes and liars and icons and agitators.

They
comment on my account about how
strong I looked next to my mother and how
ugly I am without makeup and filters
and how gross and good and brave and batshit we are.

They
believe us and they call us
liars
and they think we want fame and they think we deserve
jail. They
are certain they know us and they wonder at how little they
ever did.

They
talk about us on TV and online and in
papers
where they feature a photo of me and Mom
holding hands,
Mom gripping the notebook,
every muscle in her body
tight,
and I have the smallest, slightest
smile. They call that smile
cruel and knowing and

proud and relieved, smug and sneering and
sweet and strong.

They
pick apart the poem
like it is AP English
and they are all suddenly
scholars.

They
are
busy
but we
drink tea in the breakfast nook and watch movies from the
eighties
and order in
Thai food and burgers and breakfast for dinner
and watch Eric and his buddies lug
TVs and suitcases and boxes of
weights
out the door.

It's funny
what the truth can do,
how it can
explode your life but also make it
simpler
smaller
sweeter.

I have a hundred questions about
Walter Bruce and Betty and the boy named Dan who died in
the war,
and deeper-down questions, too,

about Eric and V-neck sweaters and skinny strapped tank tops
and also
my father and all the questions about him I've
never asked and why I've never asked them
and also
also
the photos.
The ones from the mantel and
the one
when I was thirteen
and why
she didn't
take my hand the way I took hers,
why she couldn't,
and why I could
and what that means.

But.
There is time
for answers to questions that live
deep, deep down in the fabric of us.
There is time
after our
spicy sandwiches and
Girls Just Wanna Have Fun, Dirty Dancing, Fame,
Eighties-Dance-Movie-a-thon.
There is time
after these long days
between Christmas and New Year's,
between before and after,
for that.

We turn off our phones and
don't answer the door

and we put away messages on our emails
and we ring in the new year
by writing
poems
about the things we don't understand and the things we maybe
do,
because you can't move in to the new year,
not really,
if all the old ones
haven't had a chance to
speak.

I don't know
what Mom writes, what stories she still has left
to unearth, but her pencil
scribbles and smudges and she
sighs
a lot.

I write
in the attic,
surrounded by the past,
knowing
finally
how present it
is.

And maybe there are new secrets
in those poems,
but they are
no longer
a curse. They are now
instead
a promise of things

we will say out loud

when we need to.

Mimi, 2022

Remembering Mimi, 2019

"Let's not do the whole
thing," Mom said about Christmas, meaning,
I guess,
the tree and the presents and the stockings and the

love.

We hadn't really done
the whole thing
for my birthday a few days earlier,
so I guess it wasn't a
surprise,
but it was
something.

"Eric isn't that into Christmas," she said,
about the guy
who had just started living with us.

"So we're just gonna . . ." I didn't even know
how to end the sentence. Usually Mom and I
baked cookies and sang songs about Rudolph and got each other
sweaters
and stayed in our PJs all day. Usually it was

nice.
Eric had a habit of taking something
nice
and making it
disappear. He didn't like the wind chimes out front or
Mom's curly hair or
Taco Tuesdays. He didn't like going to the bookstore on
Sundays or
the comfiest, oldest armchair in the family room.

I thought they were
pillars,
anchors,
part of the foundation holding us together. I thought
those things
were what we were built on,
Mom and I. So when he
banished them from our home,
from our lives,
I waited for everything to
crumble down. And it sort of
did,
just not the way I would have guessed.

The older kids,
the ones with shoulderless sweaters and
blue hair and
big smiles,
told me to come on by,
wrote it on my account under the picture of me
curled onto the couch watching *Elf,* pretending Mom was curled
up in the other
corner
even though she was out with Eric. So I

went. I liked the older kids, with their
nose piercings and political T-shirts and
vivid vocabulary, a hundred words for *sucks*, a thousand for
yes.

And,
okay, fine,
I put on
a red bra,
one I'd bought at some shop in the center of town
when I was feeling
gross, after some girl said I looked
ugly
in a photo online. I blamed my
breasts,
because weren't they always to blame for
everything,
and I thought a lacy bra
might
help.

I wore it under a black cotton dress,
and I wore fleece-lined dark green leggings in case it was the
kind of Christmas party
that required Christmas colors. When I got there,
though,
no one was wearing red or green and everyone was
kinda drunk, arms swinging and voices rising and a chaotic
energy that felt
scary but also,
I don't know,
better than the cool quiet of being at home with Eric and Mom.

"Hey, it's the

internet girl!" a junior guy said. He had what he probably called a
beard. I'd seen him before, stomping through the halls at school,
calling girls by their last names.
"Mimi," I said, because I didn't want to be known just as
internet girl.
"Mimi, Mimi," he said. "Have a drink. Have ten."
"One's good."
"One's a start."

His name was Randall and he
watched me drink my first
screwdriver, then poured me
another.
"How'd you get so
famous?" he asked, leaning toward me like he really
cared.
I shrugged. "I don't really
know. I wrote a post about not having a dad,
not ever asking
who he was, because it didn't matter,
he wasn't there for a reason
and I had my mom,
and it went sort of
viral,
like it was scandalous and admirable and a whole
thing
that I wasn't, like,
desperate to know my dad, that I was fine
with just my mom,
and I guess people saw my photo and thought
something about me,
and they saw my mom's photo
and remembered her from like the two movies or whatever she

did
a hundred years ago,
and
I just kept
writing stuff and posting stuff and they kept
reading it."

I was a little
breathless when I finished speaking,
and I could see on his face
that I shouldn't have really
answered
with the whole truth.
That the question
about me
and who I was
was
filler. Was not
the point.
"So you think your followers are there for your writing?"
Randall said. He
wiggled his eyebrows. He
looked like he might laugh.
"At least a little," I said.
"I think they like
the rest of you too, right?" he said. "You know you're the
best-looking girl in school
and you're only in eighth grade. That's
pretty incredible. I bet that's why you're famous
too. And your writing. I'm sure it's
good.
I've never really read
your posts, you know?" He stretched a long arm
around my shoulder. He

squeezed.
I think
I *think*
it was a compliment
that he hadn't read the words under the photos,
like,
that it was a good thing that I was so
pretty or whatever
that he
didn't care what I had to say?
I tried to make it sound
nice in my head.

Now,
though,
it sounds like total
bullshit.

I had another screwdriver and he said I should take a photo
with him for my page and I
did.
I had another, and he
told me we should take photos outside because it was starting to
snow. We did that
too;
an impromptu photo shoot
that was nothing but blurry patches of white.
Just like Clinton said,
snow is only beautiful
when you're seeing it fall with your own two eyes. That's the sort
of
thing
Randall didn't
care about.

After a fifth
screwdriver,
he told me we should take photos
upstairs.

I don't know what I said.
I remember the way my head
swam and how funny it felt to smile. I remember
looking in the mirror really hard
to try to decide something
about myself, and how the looseness of my arms made motions
feel
sexier and then
scarier.

I remember that upstairs was some guy's room.
Maybe it was Randall's?
Maybe this was Randall's house? And I remember
other people came in and I said
hi
and they
laughed. I remember unbuttoning my dress
and then not being able to
and then someone else
doing it for me.
I remember sticking out my tongue and that it felt
good, that I felt
good, that I liked being a little
out of control and I liked Randall and I liked
whoever these other people
in here
were, and I felt like I was a part of it,
even though I wasn't quite sure what

it was, and time passed and someone made me
coffee and someone else
drove me home
and I fell asleep on the couch,
I guess,
because it's where I woke up, creases on my cheeks and my
mouth all
bone-dry and
rancid.

I guess that's what high school parties
are like, I thought. And I didn't think much more
until I got online
and there it was
a photo of me
with my bra
and my tongue
and everyone saying I played all sweet and innocent online
but really I was
this.

And I couldn't understand how one night of me being
that
meant that's all I could ever be. And when Mom found
out I asked her
what to do,
asked her to call someone's parents and make them
apologize and take it down,
and maybe wasn't it illegal? And couldn't Randall get in trouble
because I didn't say yes
to these photos or at least I don't remember
saying anything
and wasn't it my body and weren't they wrong for
photographing it? And she

left the room
for an hour or two
and when she came back her eyes were
red
and she told me I need to learn to make better decisions
and that Eric was
right,
teenage girls are
trouble,
and she certainly wasn't about to call someone's mother
because I really shouldn't have put myself in that
position, and what was I doing
in a bra like that
anyway,
and it was
embarrassing for her and for
Eric
and for me and I owed
Eric an apology and her, too, and
maybe everyone.

Her voice
shook and shuddered and she
squeezed her hands into fists
like she was keeping something secret
in her palms.

"Apologize for what?" I said.
She shook her head like the answer was obvious.

After the holidays

I came back to a school full of girls
who hated me for the way their boyfriends
looked at me,
texted about me,
said what they'd like to
do to me.

"We had
fun," Randall said,
when I asked him why. He
shrugged.
People are always
shrugging
at things that matter, like their shoulders can make it all
meaningless.

"Anyway. You look good
today
too," he said like I was not teary-eyed and shaky-kneed. He
wiggled his eyebrows like we were doing something
dangerous
and flirty,
like I was wearing this shirt
just for him
or them
all of them,
and

I looked down
to see what I was wearing,
like everyone does
because no one ever remembers
what they put on in the morning,
and it was just

a black shirt,
just a shirt
on a body,
except on my body
it was never allowed to be just
a shirt.

Mimi, 2023

I don't go back to school on January 3rd or 4th or 5th.
We
hide out
like our home is a fort we've made with blankets and a
"No Boys Allowed"
sign out front.

We listen to Stephanie give
interviews on the news and we
think of her as family,
too,
the kind who used to have secrets
but don't
anymore, the kind that
believe you. I like how she pushes her glasses up on the bridge of
her nose every few words.
I like how she says Mom's name in this very serious voice,
like Mom matters, like it matters
what she read, and like it does not matter at all
what anyone else thinks of it.

"Tiffany Dovewick is a hero. She has
done her part. And now it's up to
the rest of us
to keep asking the world to change."

Our phones ring and the news
drones on about
little girls and their diaries

and powerful men and their
proclivities,
but we just hide
and wait
and try to find a place to hang on to,
because we are
untethered.

And really the only thing to hold on to
is each other.

Mimi, 2023

Meet me at the lake? I text Clinton
on the weekend.
I'll bring hot chocolate, he texts back,
like no time at all has passed,
like nothing has changed about him and me,
and
I can't help it:
I like him.
I more than like him.
I like that he is there somehow,
even now,
after everything,
after I told him not to be,
after I became a symbol of
something
with my mom,
after everything.

He's there before me,
mittened and grinning and holding
a huge thermos for us to share.

"You look good all
bundled up," he says,
and he can't possibly know
that it's the best thing I could hear.
That I'm not sure anyone has ever told me that I look good
when my body is under layers of down
and puff

and wool
and warmth.

"You do too," I say.
I'm not even really sure exactly why
we're here,
but maybe there doesn't have to be a reason.
"Lakes in winter make me
kind of sad," Clinton says.
"Oh shit, they do? I wouldn't have brought you here, but you
said—"
"Sad isn't so bad," he says, shaking his head. "Sad is—I'm not
scared of sad."
"Oh," I say. "I am."
"I used to come to the lake with my dad," he says. He says
dad
so soft I barely hear it,
which is how I know
it hurts.
"In winter?" I ask.
"Yeah. It feels like a long time ago,
but actually
we were here last winter
right before
he died."

"Oh," I say. "Wow."

"It's a good place to come
when the world is
changing," he says.

"Is it?" I ask. "Is the world changing?"

"For you, I mean, for you and your mom and
whoever else."

"All we did was say something
true. All she did, I mean.
I just stood there. In the truth. With her."

"You don't think
the truth
changes everything?" Clinton asks.

I can't come up with any answer. I am still
new to the truth;
I am still
picking up the pieces of it
and fitting them together. I still have
notebooks to read and
questions to ask my mother,
my grandmother,
maybe someday
a father,
if I decide to find out
who he is. I still have
pieces of history to stitch together
like a dress, like an enormous dress that needs to fit me just
right,
and luckily I am good at
stitches, good at piecing things together, making it all unlikely
and
beautiful.

I take Clinton's hand. It is mittened and big. It is perfect with
my mittened
hand.

I don't know if this is how Betty felt
with Peter
before it all turned awful,
but she never wrote about holding hands or
sharing secrets.

I don't know if this is how Wendy felt
with Dan
before that, too, turned
tragic.

I have the words they wrote down
but not
the whole picture. Not the whole
story. I don't know that we ever get
the whole
story.

I want to read a love story
in the notebooks,
a good one
with a happy ending,
but I'm worried there isn't one
there.

Except.
Except.
Except.

We end up sitting on the cold ground
and talking about his father's favorite songs
and my mother's favorite books
and what we think it means about who we are or who we might
someday
become.

And maybe there is no love story in the notebooks in the attic.
But maybe
there is a love story
right
here.

Mimi, 2023

Mom lets me drive.
"You've got this," she says.
We know where we're going,
sort of.
An address given to us
by a woman named Lynne who says
she finally found
her birth mother's name,
and an outdated address
on a registry of birth mothers
who wanted to be
found.
"I know she's
gone.
I wish I'd looked
sooner,
I guess she
wanted me to find her.
But I found you
instead."
Lynne sounded
surprised and glad and also
sad and scared.
She had the name
Dovewick,
and then she saw the name
on the news
and saw our blonde hair, our small bodies, our unexpected
curves, and

our squinting
blue
eyes,
and she thought
oh,
wow,
yes.
And she thought,
she said,
if we choose to believe anyone could feel this way about
us:

I hope it's them.
I'd be
proud to be
one of them.

It will take us
away
for
days that will turn into nights and back into days,
the way daughters turn into mothers, then do what their
mothers before them did,
the same but different,
the stars staying stable in the night sky
but the rest of us circling around it,
changing our position;
changing the way
we see it all.

"She might be
awful," I say. "She doesn't know the whole
story of us

or you or
me
or Betty or
Wendy or—"

"We don't know the whole story of her
either," Mom says. "And we can't stay here."
She nods her head to what we've left
behind,
a house swarmed by
reporters and photographers and people who want to tell
more of a story
that we've finished telling. They look through our
trash
and demand more
notebooks
and tell us who we
are, which is impossible because we are still trying to answer that
ourselves.

On the way, we pick up
my grandmother
Wendy,
who packed light and wears a
scowl
but is here, is curious,
is willing to
go somewhere
we haven't been before.

"You read the poem," she says
to Mom. There is no
tone of voice,
no indication of what it

means. "You read it to all those people. The whole world."

"Yep," Mom says.
"Brave," Wendy says, and again there's no
tone
underneath it;
it is a statement of
fact. It Is

the truth.

We drive and drive and

drive. We stop and eat things like milkshakes and
Chex Mix
and bananas past their prime and
Taco Bell. We tell
stories,
ones from the notebooks,
and other ones, too,
about boys we liked and people we
tried to get to like us
and reasons we wanted to be
famous and
terrible things we said
that we meant and didn't mean
and also just

what we baked during the pandemic
and where we were when we found out who won the last
election

and where Mom thinks I should go to college and why
(my grandmother thinks I should just move to New York and
work for
some fashion designer), and what they both
want me to sew for them next: something blue and flowy for my
grandmother,
something shimmery and shiny for Mom.
We talk about
what new podcast
we're listening to
and whether we think we'd rather live
near an ocean or a mountain
and whether Clinton is a good name
for a first boyfriend.

Maybe this is
family
or maybe this woman Lynne
is
or maybe we'll find it somewhere else
or maybe it is just
the notebooks,
the tradition of it,
the way they last, the way we don't rip up the pages and
burn the words
when they get messy. Maybe family is
what we've already been doing,
which is muddling through and writing it down,
which is trying to say
the truth,
or at least our version of it.

I don't know
if this is family

or if Clinton is love
or if Mom is a hero
or if I am
Mimi Dovewick or @MimiDove or the girl on the mantel or the
words in this notebook
or someone else entirely.

But the windows are open and
we take turns picking songs
and I am wearing
my green dress with Betty's pearls sewn on it
and a flannel shirt
tied at my waist
because I am past and present and
future, too,
or I am
just a girl
in a car
with her family
and it is destiny or a
revolution
or just a road trip,
who can say.

Maybe we'll know for sure
what this all is
and means
in fifty years or a hundred.
Maybe it doesn't matter until we know what it
leads to, or maybe
it

matters
all on its own.

Lila Betty, 2054

The notebook is blue,
and inside are three poems
in my mother's curvy, swervy handwriting.

"Here," she says. "Happy birthday."

"What is it?" I ask.
"A space to write," Mom says. "A lawless space."
"Lawless?"
"Sure," she says. "You know, a space that no one can tell you
what to do
or who to be. A place just for you. No rules."
"What would I write?" I ask.
"Your story," she says, like it's that simple,
and maybe it is.

Maybe
it
is.

Dear Reader,

The topics covered in this book—particularly those around sexual trauma—are all too common and are incredibly difficult, complicated, and overwhelming things to engage with. Though I hope this book offers moments of connection and the opportunity for readers who need it to be seen, other support is out there, and whatever your experience, you deserve to be heard and supported.

The sexual assault, harassment, and trauma I have gone through in my own life has sometimes felt confusing or unclear or maybe even not worthy of further discussion or help. But what I have learned through sharing my story and going to therapy and engaging with resources aimed toward survivors of all forms of sexual trauma is that there is no invisible standard of worthiness or realness. If you feel that you have been violated in any way, you deserve support and help for working through that reality.

The most important thing to know is that it is never your fault. You are not bad, and the trauma you have endured is not because of anything you did. Consent can feel like something you have given, simply because you didn't say no, but it's important to know that anything less than enthusiastic, sober consent is not consent.

If you would like further resources, beyond the trusted adults in your community, RAINN is a great place to start. Their website is https://www.rainn.org/ and their free hotline is 1 (800) 656-HOPE.

Take care of yourselves, believe survivors, and believe your own experiences.

With love and care,
Corey

Acknowledgments

This is the longest a book has ever taken me to write. I have been working on *Lawless Spaces* for six years in many different forms and with a million different ideas of what it would ultimately be. A lot of people helped it take this shape.

Thank you to my editor, Nicole Ellul, whose smart and thoughtful and compassionate work on this story helped me find a heart, a direction, a center that I struggled for years to locate. I am so grateful to you for being on this journey, in this time, on this book, with me.

Thank you to Jennifer Ung, whose thoughts and encouragement and connection helped me better understand what this story was about and why I needed to tell it. I feel so lucky we connected while working on this book.

Thank you as always to Victoria Marini for years of support, and especially for supporting this book in even its strangest, least sensical forms. Your saying yes to my big, wild, risky ideas makes me a better writer, and inspires me to say yes to myself too.

Thank you to Liesa Abrams for getting it, for seeing it, and for making a path forward for this book. Thank you for initial nudges and thoughts that helped give shape to a messy manuscript. You make me brave.

Thank you to the wonderful authenticity readers who gave their time and hearts to this book. Your thoughts were indispensable, and I am honored you shared so much of yourselves.

And a hearty and bighearted thank you to everyone at Simon & Schuster Books for Young Readers who put their hearts and minds and creative energies toward this book. Thank you especially to Amanda Ramirez, Sara Berko, Morgan York, Marinda Valenti, Stephanie Evans Biggins, Krista Vossen, Emma Leonard, and Tom Daly.